"I Want You to Leave Me Alone!"

"What's the matter with you? Do you think it's more exciting to resist?" He leaned across to take her hands in his, and looked into her eyes in a way that was so appealing she almost forgot her protest.

"You've made a terrible mistake. You don't know me; you don't know what kind of a girl I am."

"I know exactly what kind of a girl you are. So don't play the innocent. Why not cooperate and make this little business junket of ours more pleasant for both of us?"

MEREDITH LINDLEY,

a third generation Californian, enjoys a unique first-hand opportunity to study romance behind the scenes. She has worked for television and film and is currently writing a movie treatment for a romantic comedy.

Dear Reader:

Silhouette Books is pleased to announce the creation of a new line of contemporary romances—*Silhouette Special Editions*. Each month we'll bring you six new love stories written by the best of today's authors— Janet Dailey, Brooke Hastings, Laura Hardy, Sondra Stanford, Linda Shaw, Patti Beckman, and many others.

Silhouette Special Editions are written with American women in mind; they are for readers who want more: more story, more details and descriptions, more realism, and more *romance*. *Special Editions* are longer than most contemporary romances allowing for a closer look at the relationship between hero and heroine with emphasis on heightened romantic tension and greater sensuous and sensual detail. If you want more from a romance, be sure to look for *Silhouette Special Editions* on sale this February wherever you buy books.

We welcome any suggestions or comments, and I invite you to write us at the address below.

Karen Solem
Editor-in-Chief
Silhouette Books
P.O. Box 769
New York, N. Y. 10019

MEREDITH LINDLEY
Against the Wind

Silhouette *Romance*

Published by Silhouette Books New York

America's Publisher of Contemporary Romance

For Helen

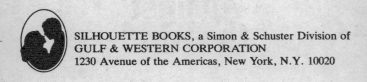

SILHOUETTE BOOKS, a Simon & Schuster Division of
GULF & WESTERN CORPORATION
1230 Avenue of the Americas, New York, N.Y. 10020

ISBN: 0-671-57116-8

First Silhouette Books printing November, 1981

10 9 8 7 6 5 4 3 2 1

America's Publisher of Contemporary Romance

Printed in the U.S.A.

Chapter One

Molly walked carefully along the dock, watching her every step for fear of catching a slender heel in the wide spaces between the boards. She stopped for a moment to consult the slip of newspaper in her hand.

FOR SALE: 36-foot sloop in excellent condition. Sterling Yacht Brokerage, Marina Del Rey.

Mr. Gunther had spotted the ad just this morning, and insisted she check it out for him right away, without allowing her time to change into clothing more convenient for sailboat shopping. Now she felt conspicuous in her matte jersey dress with the gold chains around her neck where jeans and sweatshirts were the uniform of the day.

She took a moment to look around her. In every

direction as far as she could see there were boats of all sizes bobbing in the water. There were enough boats tied to this one dock alone to completely fill the small harbor in Massachusetts where she had learned to sail as a youngster. And this was just one small inlet out of a marina as big as her whole hometown. She wondered if she would ever get used to the opulent proportions of everything in Southern California.

"Looking for someone?"

The sound of the abrasive masculine voice jarred her, and she spun around to see a man's head emerging from the hatch of a beautiful sailboat in the slip behind her. She recognized it as a sloop of about thirty-six feet in length, and she was relieved that she had happened upon the very boat she was looking for.

"I'm here about the ad in the paper this morning. I'd like to come aboard and look around. . . ."

As she spoke the man ascended the steps up onto the deck, and he seemed to grow giant-sized before her eyes. He towered over her as the height of the deck was added to his own height of well over six feet. He was wearing a knit watch cap over his curly blond hair, and a faded T-shirt that once had been Navy-issue blue. His jeans had obviously been washed to such a point of softness that they formed themselves like a second layer of skin around the rounded hard musculature of his legs.

"You're not stepping on this deck in those shoes," he announced, his eyes sweeping over her with insolence. She was uncomfortably aware of his appraising look, which seemed to reach out to touch and measure every curve of her body beneath the pale green fabric of her dress as it rippled slightly in the sea breeze. She took a deep breath to calm herself, then looked into his eyes and said with quiet firmness, "I'm sure the owner won't mind if a potential customer looks around."

The deckhand put down the bucket of varnish and paintbrush he was carrying with an impatient shrug, clearly exhibiting his displeasure at being interrupted in his work. Then he stared at her with a stubborn look that stiffened his square jawline. He made no move to help her, and she sensed from his arrogant attitude that he was one of those workmen who had been given just enough authority to enjoy acting the tyrant.

She decided to comply with his request, but only because she knew he was within his right to demand it. It would be a shame to mar the perfection of the teak decking that glowed with a burnished luster that only loving hands could have bestowed upon it. She reached down and unfastened the black patent leather sandals, kicking them off with a nonchalant gesture that she hoped would show she had surrendered none of her purposefulness with her obedience to him.

She stepped up onto the deck of the boat quickly so that she wouldn't have to accept his extended hand, but her stockinged foot did not give her the firm grip of a rubber deck shoe, and almost at once she felt herself begin to slip slightly. Before she could reach out to take hold of the nearest stanchion to steady herself, he stepped toward her and grabbed her around the waist so abruptly that he pulled her off balance and she fell into his arms.

"Would you put me down? I can manage all right," she protested.

He laughed, his lips so close to her hair that the sardonic sound of it rang in her ears, then carried her effortlessly toward the cockpit and dumped her down on the cushions.

Molly adjusted the folds of her dress and then

hurried to make their relationship more business-like. "Tell me what you know about this boat," she said.

"She's a real love," he drawled. "Just the kind I like. Like a good woman she's always full of spirit, ready for action, and she responds right away to good rough handling."

Molly looked at him dubiously, realizing he was teasing her with his double entendres.

"I mean, how is she built?" Molly asked, regretting her choice of words almost at once.

"She's beautifully built," he said, leaning back against the superstructure and scrutinizing her again through half-closed eyes. His look moved up and down her body as he spoke. "She's wide of beam, and just a little bit top-heavy, but she gives a man a heck of a ride."

Molly's hand fluttered nervously to the neckline of her dress, where she adjusted the surplice crossing of fabric that stretched across the high curve of her bosom. She was grateful she had enough self-control to resist the impulse she felt to jump up and slap him in the face. Instead she turned away from him to hide her humiliated embarrassment. But he seemed to have tired of the game, and now he turned his attention to the subject matter at hand.

"She's completely rigged for single-handed sailing. She's got self-tailing winches, double preventors and a furling jib."

"I see."

"But I suppose you're more interested in the galley and the cabin space," he said.

"As a matter of fact, I would like to take a look down below."

"Be my guest," he said, extending one tanned arm toward the open companionway just in front of them.

She made her way carefully down the three steep steps into the main salon. It took her eyes a moment or two to adjust to the dark after the bright sunlight outside. Then she regarded the cozy interior with open awe. Every inch glowed with the warm reflection of well-oiled wood. Beneath her bare feet a deep pile carpet of a lighter beige softened her steps. The settee was upholstered in a heavy fabric with a brown and blue flame-stitch design on it, and along the oversized side windows expensive lined curtains in a woven fabric of dark blue were set in a sliding track. Here and there the burnished glow of brass fittings and accessories added to the luxury.

"Right here on the port side is the galley," she heard a voice behind her say, and then she realized with a start that the rude deckhand had followed her down the companionway ladder into the cabin area. Standing before him with her shoes off she felt that he loomed over her like an oncoming tidal wave. He pointed out the stainless steel gimbaled stove and the double sinks, and she noticed the beautiful leaded glass doors on a liquor locker, which was obviously well-stocked with wine.

"And she shall have music wherever she goes," he said, flipping a switch that filled the cabin with music from a built-in stereo system. "Shall we dance?" He wiped his paint-stained hands down the thighs of his jeans and held his arms out toward her.

"Whoever owns this boat certainly has a craving for the creature comforts," she said shortly, ignoring his gesture.

"Glad you mentioned comfort," he said, moving toward the intricately carved door at the forward end of the salon. "This is where the captain sleeps," he said, throwing open the door.

She stepped inside to look at the sumptuous cabin. The paneling was a rich mahogany color, held in

place with polished strips of brass. A berth took up
most of the space, and a fur throw was tossed over it
as a bedspread. A small porthole had been fitted
with a piece of stained glass that filtered a sensuous
stream of multicolored light inside.

"Notice the Plexiglas hatch over your head. From
this berth you can watch the stars overhead all night
long. Am I tempting you?" he asked, bending
toward her to give a salacious wink.

The man was beginning to get on her nerves, and
she felt the first slight tingle of fear as she realized
that she was trapped on board this boat, with his
huge bulk between her and the only exit.

He squeezed past her to step into the room,
pausing just long enough for her to feel the strong
masculinity of his body pressed close to hers in the
small doorjamb. Before she could recover her as-
saulted senses enough to get away from him, he
grabbed her wrist and twisted it so that she was
forced over to the berth. With another painful twist
he pulled her down to sit beside him.

"You'd better try this. After all, if you aren't
happy in the bunk, you won't be happy anywhere on
board."

"As a matter of fact, there is no point in looking
any further. I don't think this boat is what we want."

He reached up slowly to pull the knit cap from his
head, releasing the mass of curly blond hair that she
noticed was badly in need of a trim. She was
repulsed by his crude manner and his intimate
insinuations. All she could think of now was making
her escape from him, but he had moved his strong
brown hand from her wrist down to the fingers of her
left hand.

"We? The boat is not what 'we' want? Are you
shopping for a honeymoon boat?" he said, studying
the slender ringless fingers of her hand.

"I am looking for a boat on behalf of my boss, Mr. Leland Gunther. He is a very busy man and he doesn't have time to waste in shopping around, so he has asked me to find him something suitable."

"So you're not just a dockside groupie."

"A what?"

"I thought you were just one of those beautiful girls who hangs around the marina all decked out and looking for a rich guy with a boat to attract."

"Now you have gone too far," she said, pulling her hand from his grasp and standing up. She could feel her face begin to flush with anger. "I'm going to see to it that you never get another job at this marina."

"The very powerful Mr. Gunther has taught you how to throw your weight around, has he?" the man said, following her into the salon. "Well, this time you've met your match," he chuckled.

"I'm going to discuss this with the owner of this boat, as well as the owner of this anchorage," she said.

"The owner of the Sterling Yacht Brokerage is Brett Sterling. He also owns this boat."

"I've heard his name, I know who he is."

"Do you also know that he owns that apartment complex over there?" he said nodding toward shore.

"I'm sure he'll want to hear what I have to say."

"He's listening."

"What?"

"I said he's listening right now to what you have to say."

Suddenly the young man pulled up his T-shirt, exposing most of his tanned chest in the process. But what he was trying to call to her attention was the silver buckle on the belt around his waist.

"My initials, see? I'm Brett Sterling."

She forced herself to pull her gaze downward from

the massive chest, covered with a fine layer of the same blond curly hair as his head. She stared at the initials on the belt buckle.

"How appropriate," she snapped.

"So you see," he said, pulling his shirt back down into place and throwing himself on the sofa, "If your Mr. Gunther wants a boat, I'm the one you'll have to deal with, insults and all."

Molly stood dumbly trying to assimilate the startling news.

Then he said, "Come and sit down here and introduce yourself and let's talk business."

"I'm sorry," she stammered. "My name is Molly Weston."

Just as she started to sit down he said, "Oh, I forgot to tell you during my tour, Molly. This settee makes up into a bed, too," and he leaned toward her with an ingratiating smile. "In case all this business talk begins to bore us."

"Now stop that. You're doing it again!" she protested hotly. "I thought I told you, I'm not one of those dockside groupies. I'm an executive secretary to a very important man, and I'm here to discuss the purchase of a boat."

This man, whether he was an ignorant deckhand or the famous Brett Sterling, still had the power to disconcert her at every turn. Why, she wondered, as she sat down, did Mr. Gunther have to put her in this position? Why couldn't he have come down here himself to look at the boat? Working for him had been a challenge for her from the first day she arrived in California: meeting his important friends, keeping track of his social life and his complicated business affairs. But this assignment had been the worst so far, and she was not at all sure that she could follow through on it.

"Perhaps you'll feel safer if we sit outside," Brett

Sterling said, springing up with a sudden tense explosion of movement that gave her a hint as to the volatile nature of his changing moods. He had disappeared up the steps into the sunlight before she could even stand up.

When she emerged into the cockpit area, she found him sitting on the bright blue vinyl cushions polishing a brass fitting.

She sat down across from him and said nothing for a few moments as she collected herself. She concentrated on the soft warm June breeze that ruffled at her hair, and the consoling caress of the bright sunlight on her face.

"I don't know why anyone would send a landlubber like you to choose a boat for him," he grumbled almost to himself as he worked.

"Now what makes you think I'm a landlubber?" she asked.

"First, you came to the marina dressed for a party. And second, it's been my experience that redheads don't like the sun so they don't care much for sailing."

"I'm not a redhead," she shot back at him, brushing her windswept pageboy into place.

"You look like it to me."

"My mother is a true redhead. My hair is brown."

"Well in the sunlight it looks red. And your skin is fair like a redhead's." He tossed her a big floppy poplin hat that had been rolled up on the cushion beside him. "You'd better put this on, you probably freckle."

"Yes, as a matter of fact I do and I don't care." She threw the hat back at him. "Now could we get back to what we're supposed to be discussing."

"All right. What kind of a boat does Mr. Gunther want?"

"Well, I don't think this one is right for him."

"This one isn't for sale anyway. The ad referred to one that's up in dry dock in my boatyard."

"I think he will want a larger boat, one he can live aboard for a few days now and then when he needs a change. And it doesn't have to be one that he can sail by himself. He'll probably want to hire a crew."

"I see. Another landlubber!"

"No he isn't. When he was younger, he did a lot of sailing."

"Well, before I can find him a boat I need to know exactly what he wants."

Molly glanced down at her watch. "Oh, look at the time. I'm supposed to meet him for dinner at six-thirty and it's almost six now."

"Where are you meeting him?" Brett asked her, putting down the polishing cloth.

"At the Fiasco right here at the marina. I'm to give him a report on what I've found so far."

Brett leaped up from where he was sitting and Molly watched him with wide startled eyes as he pulled the T-shirt off over his head, again exposing his wide chest.

"I'm going with you. You just wait a minute while I change." He called over his shoulder as he disappeared down the companionway, "There's no point in discussing this with an intermediary when I can ask him directly what it is he wants."

So, the very important Mr. Sterling had dismissed her as unnecessary. Apparently he was a man's-man, one who considered secretaries and assistants, and women in general, powerless and not worth bothering with. Well, perhaps it was just as well. Now she could get the two of them together and she could gracefully bow out of any further contacts with the haughty and contemptuous man who had made such a fool of her by pretending to be a mere swabbie on a boat that was actually his own personal yacht.

As she stepped over the side of the boat onto the dock she remembered her comment to him, criticizing the boat's owner for all the luxurious comforts on board. He could have told her right then who he was, she thought angrily. She put her shoes on, grateful that she would now be three inches taller, three inches closer to his eye level, and perhaps three inches closer to the level of importance he seemed to demand.

While she waited she moved about on the dock to regard his boat from all angles. It was a gorgeous vessel, just like one she had dreamed of having when she piloted her tiny skiff through the cold New England waters all those years ago. The color of the hull was not what she would have chosen, but the layers of shiny black paint gave the vessel a dramatic quality and made its length seem endless as it reflected sunbeams from the water. Then as she moved toward the stern she noticed the jaunty lettering across the transsept that spelled out the name of Brett Sterling's pride and joy: *Pleasure Seeker*. Appropriate, she mused bitterly, just like his initials.

She tried to imagine what the hard-bitten sailors from her hometown would think of a black sloop that came equipped with a wine rack, stereo music and a king-size bed. Extravagant, they'd call it. Too danged gaudy! Indeed, Mr. Sterling was a pleasure seeker, and one with the money to buy whatever would give him the sensual joys he was seeking.

It rankled her mind to consider the type of parties and excursions for which he probably utilized the *Pleasure Seeker*. The hat he'd offered her obviously belonged to a woman, and she was sure that if she'd looked, she would have found evidence left behind by countless female guests who had sought and found pleasure with Brett Sterling on board this craft. A man that handsome would have no trouble. . . .

"See, that didn't take long," Brett's voice interrupted the amorous visions that were floating through her head, and she blushed in spite of herself.

Brett now looked like the prosperous young businessman that he was. He had wet-combed his unruly hair into some semblance of order, and the slanting rays of the evening sun cast sparkles on the beads of water that still clung to his blond curls. His gray slacks and open-necked white silk shirt were simple but obviously expensive, and he fit as comfortably into this new role as he had into the subservient role in which she had first encountered him.

They took her car but he insisted upon driving it, apparently in fear of entrusting his life to a woman behind the wheel. When they arrived at the restaurant, Molly looked around the parking lot in vain for Mr. Gunther's car and driver, and she remembered with a stab of worry that Leland had not been feeling well this morning. It was not like him to be late to any appointment, even a dinner meeting with her, and she hoped that it wasn't illness that had detained him. He had been troubled with some bouts of irregular heartbeat, but he was in the hands of the top cardiologist in Los Angeles, so she knew she shouldn't be concerned.

Brett guided her into the restaurant with a firm hand on her back, and then left her to go put his name in for a table, requesting one at a window with a view of the harbor.

"Let's go into the bar while we wait," he whispered close to Molly's ear. "I think you could use a drink."

From then on their conversation had to be shouted above the din in the bar area where dozens of young single people were enjoying the free hors d'oeuvres. Again Brett guided her through the throng, steering her toward a far corner where one barstool stood available in a semicircular stand-up booth.

"You sit down here," he said patting the tall stool. "Maybe this will raise you up to my level where I can get a good look into those pretty brown eyes."

Molly smiled tentatively at Brett's flattery.

"How about a Pina Colada? That's what I'm going to have."

"That's fine," she said, wondering why his attitude toward her was now so gracious. Had he decided that she was a link to Mr. Gunther, who could be a very profitable customer for his yacht brokerage?

While he went to the bar to collect their drinks she regarded the people around her thoughtfully. All the sleek young women with their hair expensively cut in the latest style, and the tanned men who were trying so hard to seem outgoing and full of fun, pursued each other with an intensity that bewildered Molly. They were all dressed in vaguely nautical clothing, as if to validate their reasons for being at the marina, and to give them that mutual enthusiasm for boating on which they could build relationships. Forced laughter peeled out from all around her.

When Brett returned, he took note of the contemplative way she was observing those around her. "You seem to have made a quiet corner for us in the midst of this zoo." He put the drinks down to take her by the waist and swivel her on the stool so that she faced him, and they were indeed a bit apart from the noise.

She took the tall glass in both of her hands and began to sip the sweet coconut-flavored drink, but Brett kept one hand free to stroke it gently up and down the sleeve of her dress as he talked to her. From time to time he leaned close to her to whisper something in her ear, and she noticed the envious glance of a pretty brunette nearby who obviously thought Molly had landed a gorgeous hunk of man for the evening.

If only she knew, Molly thought wryly. *He's only being a super-salesman, trying to sell a yacht to one of the most wealthy men in Los Angeles, and using me in the process.*

"I ran away after six months in college and joined the Navy," he was saying. "Made my father so mad he wouldn't speak to me for years. But it made a man of me. And I found out that no matter what I did after that, I'd always have to find a way to own a boat. I'm most happy when I have a keel under me. It's almost better than a woman," he laughed, putting his arm around her shoulders intimately to share the joke with her. He clearly liked the feel of a woman just as much as that of a sloop.

"I know what you mean. I think Mr. Gunther feels the same way. He's not very happy right now and I think he wants a boat because—"

"Do we have to talk about Mr. Gunther? He'll be here soon enough. Let's use this time to talk about me. And you." His blue eyes seemed light and bottomless even in the murky dimness of the room as he stared into her eyes suggestively. But Molly felt a purely physical response to his closeness and his flirtation. Her mind kept telling her to draw back from him, that he was not sincere. He had already shown his true feelings toward her when he'd contemptuously called her a landlubber and insinuated she was broad of beam.

"Do you mind, you're mussing my dress," she said, reaching up to remove his hand from her shoulder.

"Well, well. Aren't we the prim one," he said, and though the words were malicious he still smiled as if he found her delightful in spite of her silly hangup. "I didn't think there was a prudish girl left in L.A. County."

"You are embarrassing me."

"Molly, there are some women who just look so darned touchable you can't keep your hands off them. You happen to be one of them."

"I—I am?"

"Yes you are. You're downright cuddly," he said, the laughter in his voice making his words loud enough that Molly was sure everyone in the room had heard him. In an effort to avoid looking at him, Molly glanced around the room, and it was with an overwhelming feeling of relief that she spotted Mr. Gunther in the doorway looking for her.

"There's Mr. Gunther now," she said shakily. "I'll go get him." Molly slid off the barstool and hurried through the throng, glad to be away from the powerful charm of Brett Sterling.

She kept her eyes on Mr. Gunther's shaggy head of white hair, which loomed above the crowd. This evening his thin shoulders seemed a bit stooped and Molly was reminded of her earlier worries about him. But when he saw her emerge from the crowded bar, his face broke into a smile.

"There you are, child. I thought you'd been swallowed up in that den of iniquity."

"Are you all right? I was worried when you were late."

Leland reached down to give her an affectionate

embrace. "Aren't you the sweet one! You're the only person left in the world now who gives a hoot how I feel. No, I'm fine."

"I've brought someone along to join us, I hope you don't mind. He deals in boats, and I think he can find you exactly what you want."

The hostess nearby called out, "Sterling, table of three."

"Oh, good, our table's ready," she said.

"Sterling. You mean Mr. Brett Sterling of Sterling Enterprises and Sterling Towers?"

At Molly's shy nod Mr. Gunther continued, "Well, little girl, you're moving in pretty fast company. Your friend doesn't just deal in boats. He owns half of the marina, I think."

"He's not my friend and he's not likely to become one. I just met him a couple of hours ago," she was quick to explain.

"Well, I marvel at how clever you are to line me up with a man like that. I don't know what I'd do without you, Molly." And with that Leland bent down to kiss Molly's cheek.

"Excuse me for interrupting this tender scene, but some of us would rather eat than smooch."

Molly spun around to see Brett, his tall frame casually propped against the wall as he regarded the two of them with a sour look. How suddenly his mood had shifted again. His snide comment made her introduction of the two men rather strained.

"Mr. Gunther, this is Brett Sterling. Brett, I'd like you to meet my employer, Leland Gunther."

"Don't believe I've had the pleasure of meeting you before, young man, but I knew your father some years ago," Leland said, extending his hand, but Brett spun away from him, leaving the older man with his hand in midair.

"Our table is ready," said Brett, as he walked off to follow the hostess.

Brett said very little during dinner. Mr. Gunther was given to long and rambling accounts of the good old days of the past, and Brett gave him rather absent attention. Molly concentrated on her plate of fettuccine and the Chicken Galliano she'd chosen as her main course, and looked out the window down a long boat-lined corridor of water that led to the main channel.

The day descended deeper and deeper into darkness, changing the panorama in the picture window. A bit of light on a dock was joined by a bulb left burning in the cabin of someone's boat, and then by the running lights on some venturesome night boater, until the view by their table revealed only inky blackness punctuated with a smattering of lights.

Molly had heard Mr. Gunther's account of his favorite weekend sail to Santa Cruz Island, and about the time he almost fell overboard during a sailboat race off Corona del Mar. She knew where every "Oh, really?" and "My goodness!" was required of the listener, so that her responses were automatic and she was left with time to think about the blond young man across the table from her who was avoiding her eyes. His attitude toward Mr. Gunther was almost hostile. He was certainly not trying to exert any salesmanship, unless he had perfected some new method of letting the client sell himself.

As the meal ended Brett pushed his chair back a bit and said to Mr. Gunther, "I think you should take time to think before you invest in the kind of boat you're talking about. When you get into those 50- or 60-foot boats, it takes a trained crew to sail them. Then you've lost all the fun of it."

"No, Mr. Sterling. I've gotten too old to do the sailing myself. But I haven't lost my sense of fun. Molly, here, was the one who suggested a sailboat."

"Oh, was she?"

"She told me I could relax on a boat, away from phones and meetings."

"Away from all distractions, with only Molly to concentrate on."

"Yes, Molly could come down and work with me on the boat. I think she'd like that."

"And whatever Molly likes, Molly gets, is that it?" Brett talked as if Molly herself were not at the table, leveling his comments about her directly at Mr. Gunther with a thin-lipped smile of forced humor playing about his lips. Mr. Gunther either did not notice Brett's disdainful attitude, or was too gentlemanly to give it consideration.

"Well, Mr. Gunther, it seems to me you're getting into boat ownership for all the wrong reasons. If you've owned a boat before, you know you shouldn't buy one on the basis of someone's whim." With those words Brett directed his glance at Molly for the first time since they'd sat down at the table. "It has to be because you really want to do it."

"Young man, all this talk of sea adventures has worn me out. I'm afraid I'm going to have to cut this evening short," Mr. Gunther said, laying his napkin aside and reaching into his suit jacket for his wallet.

Molly asked him, "Are you feeling all right?"

"Yes, of course I am. I just don't have the stamina of you two young people. Here, Molly, use this to pay for our dinner." He tossed a credit card to her but Brett lunged across the table to intercept it and toss it back to Mr. Gunther.

"I'll take care of it, Mr. Gunther," Brett said with a tone that brooked no argument.

"Thank you, son, that's real nice. I will return the favor someday. Molly, dear, you be careful driving home by yourself. Which car did you bring?"

"The Buick."

"Well, you just leave it in the driveway when you get home. I want Perkins to have it serviced. You can use the Mercedes the rest of the week."

"Thank you, Mr. Gunther, and good-night."

She watched Mr. Gunther weave his lanky frame through the tables toward the door with an affectionate smile on her face. It was hard to believe that she had once considered him to be a ruthless businessman. That was when he had been a business associate of her father's. Her mother probably still believed that Mr. Gunther had been responsible for all her father's financial woes. But since Mr. Gunther had sent for her to come to California and serve as his secretary, she had come to know him well. She admired his sound business ethics and his concern for his employees.

"He's a generous man, your Mr. Gunther."

She turned her attention back to the brooding man across from her. He was sprinkling colored sugar crystals into his coffee, again avoiding her eyes.

"Yes, he is. He's the greatest."

"He'd do almost anything for you, wouldn't he?"

"Yes, I think he would."

"But you pay a high price for that kind of devotion."

"I suppose so. I work hard, my hours aren't my own. He gives me some very difficult assignments."

She stopped to consider the current vexing situation Mr. Gunther had gotten her into. Thank goodness her contact with the moody Mr. Sterling was almost at an end.

"I don't know how you can do it."

"We New England girls were brought up to enjoy hard work," she said, trying to lighten the mood. "I suppose I should get going, I have a long drive."

"Where do you—where does Mr. Gunther live?"

"Oh, he has a beautiful home in Hancock Park. I live in the guesthouse over the garage. It's very convenient to his office, he works from his home."

"And very discreet. You New England girls have such a sense of decorum."

Molly wondered what had happened to the flirtatious man who had given her so much concentrated attention just before dinner. He was now blurting out his cryptic comments while summoning the waitress with a wave, and searching his back pocket for his wallet. He seemed anxious to end the evening and be rid of her.

Brett drove her car back to the Sterling Yacht Brokerage docks without saying another word. She imagined that he was angry with himself for talking Mr. Gunther out of buying a boat. He had spoiled a potentially big sale by unleashing his bad humor at just the wrong time, and she was sure he knew it.

"Good-night, and thank you for dinner," she said politely as he opened the car door for her. He walked beside her around the car to let her into the driver's side. But before she could reach out for the door handle he reached out roughly for her hand and stopped her. He pulled her around to face him, and then pressed himself against her with such force that her body was backed tightly against the side of the car.

He stared down into her eyes for just an instant, and the bright orange lights of the parking lot lit up his face, giving it a demoniacal intensity that frightened her. Then he kissed her, not the way Todd had kissed her after the senior prom, or the way Alex had kissed her that evening during the fireworks display in the Town Square at home. This kiss was full of anger. He forced himself between her reluctant lips with an urgency that insisted upon response. But she held herself rigid, crushed against the car by the total hard weight of his body against hers.

Then, quite distinctly, she could feel a change in him, signified by a wave of relaxation that rippled down his length. He released his bruising grip on her shoulders to wrap his arms around her, caressing her back with a touch that was almost gentle. His lips against hers were now soft and searching. In spite of herself she could feel a surge of excitement. Her tense fingers uncurled from their tightly fisted position. No longer weapons, they became instruments of exploration. She put her hands behind his neck, and as his kiss slowly ebbed away from her, she relished the feel of the soft curling hair where it met his shirt collar.

"You're very good at that," he said, after clearing his throat slightly as if he could hardly get the words out. But before she could release the smile that was playing at the edges of her still-parted lips, he spoke again.

"It comes with practice, I guess. You're a professional."

Molly stopped her smile before it had fully blossomed. She did not know whether to laugh or to cry.

"Good-night," he said, suddenly moving away from her across the parking lot, loping toward the docks and his beloved *Pleasure Seeker*.

During the long drive down the dark freeways that led her away from the sea Molly rubbed her tongue across her bruised lips and forced herself to breathe with an even rhythm until she was calm.

She noticed the light on in Mr. Gunther's room as she drove down the curving driveway past his brick colonial home and toward her guest apartment at

the back of the large piece of property. She felt
sheltered and protected living here, knowing Leland
was just a shout away, that she was in his care. And
on this night, more than ever, she appreciated it.

The next morning she walked across the back lawn
to the outside entrance into Mr. Gunther's study. He
was a marvel, already at work placing calls to his
investment counselors in the east where it was nearly
lunchtime. She tried to force a bright look for him in
spite of the heavy pall over her emotions that her
evening at the marina had left with her.

"I wanted to see you before I take off for my
handball session at the club," Leland boomed.
"That Mr. Sterling called this morning. I set up an
appointment for you at eleven o'clock."

"He what? You what?"

"Says he's got a list of candidates for us to look
over, boats I might like. So you go on down there
and see what you think. If there's one on the list that
you like, I'll take a look at it later this week."

"But, Mr. Gunther, I thought he'd convinced you,
I thought you'd decided to forget the whole thing.
And he certainly didn't seem interested last night in
helping you find your dream boat."

"I'm still determined to have a boat beside me to
comfort me in my old age." He patted his pockets
and ruffled through the papers on his desk. "Now
where did I put that? Oh, here it is. Penthouse
Office, Sterling Towers. You know where that is.
Eleven o'clock. And for heaven's sake put on some
more lipstick before you go. You look pale as a ghost
this morning."

Chapter Two

A denim skirt landed on the wicker rocking chair, a pair of corduroy slacks fell behind the door, a cotton dress was forgotten, spread out on the bed, as Molly dressed for her meeting. Remembering the "casual-chic" of most of the marina girls at the restaurant last night, she finally settled on a blue chambray skirt with a matching shirtblouse, and tied the sleeves of a crew-necked Shetland sweater around her neck over it, checking her outline in the mirror to make sure the effect was not too "top-heavy." She was determined not to appear as overdressed as she had yesterday in her office clothes. She wanted to give Mr. Sterling no motivation for his teasing. This was to be a short and simple business encounter.

She parked Mr. Gunther's Mercedes in the beautifully landscaped parking circle in front of the Sterling Towers apartment complex. A lobby sign directed her to the special elevator that serviced only the penthouse and she shot up twelve floors before she had time to plan the opening remarks with which she hoped to defang Mr. Sterling.

Molly expected Brett's penthouse office to be presided over by a snooty secretary, backed by a chorus of docile but gorgeous typists and stenographers. So when the door opened, she was rather startled to be greeted by a bear of a man wearing a tank-top that exposed colorful tattoos on both of his slightly drooping biceps.

"Greetings, matey. I'm McKenzie, everyone just calls me Mac for short. And you'd be Miss Molly Weston, I suppose."

"I have an appointment with Mr. Sterling. For eleven o'clock. Is this his office?"

"His office, his homeport, his boarding house, whatever you want to call it. Come right along, he's waiting for you."

Molly followed him across the foyer and through tall oak doors that opened into a bright open space. The entire western exposure of the room was glass, which opened the area to a dramatic view across a broad terrace to all of the marina below, and then the Pacific Ocean's endless horizon beyond.

The room was richly carpeted in an earthy gold tone, but was furnished almost entirely in contemporary Lucite furniture, so that the chair cushions and potted plants and tabletop accessories appeared to float in the rarefied atmosphere.

Remembering the cluttered desks behind which she and Mr. Gunther worked and her humming typewriter and peeling telephone, Molly wondered where the vast Sterling empire was administered. Surely secreted behind a door somewhere there was a practical office. But the quick glance she cast through an open doorway they passed only revealed a bedroom, again with a full glass wall facing the view. This was, then, Brett Sterling's home, at least when he wasn't down at the dock seeking pleasure on the *Pleasure Seeker*. How she wished he had chosen a more neutral ground on which to conduct their meeting!

"Right out there on the patio, Missy. Through that sliding glass door. Cap'n Brett thought it was such a beautiful day and all. It's flying fish weather, sure to tell."

After casting an experienced eye across the horizon to make his weather report, McKenzie rolled away from her with the side-to-side gait obviously adopted after years of walking a deck, and disappeared.

Molly went out onto the wide terrace, and picked the closest grouping of chairs around a table. She sat down and removed a notebook and pencil from her purse and arranged them precisely before her on the table so that she was ready for work.

"I can't very well talk to you way over there," Brett called out to her with his unmistakably imperious tone.

Molly looked around her in all directions and she could see no one. At the farthest edge of the patio there was an area set apart with a circle of small shrubs planted in pots as big as kettledrums. Perhaps he was behind that foliage she decided, and she got up with a sigh, knowing she was expected to go to him and not vice versa.

She rounded the row of plants with a confident enough spring to her step, but what she saw at that point made her leap back a step or two with an involuntary reaction of shock. Here on the outermost corner of the terrace, submerged into the redwood decking, was a whirlpool spa big enough to bathe an elephant in. And lounging beneath the bubbling, swirling water was Brett Sterling, his head thrown back against the tile edge of the hot tub, his eyes closed with proper worshipful respect to the sun.

From her hiding place behind the ficus tree where she had jumped, Molly gave serious consideration to running for the door, but then she heard a sharp command.

"Come on over here where I can talk to you."

Molly stepped forward cautiously, trying to appear undisturbed by the unusual turn this meeting was taking. Brett opened his eyes and his lips moved in a mocking smile as he watched her edging toward him.

"I came here to discuss business," she said forcing equilibrium into her voice.

"Then let's get to it," he responded. "We have available to us a computerized boat search, I don't know if you're aware of that. I programmed all of Mr. Gunther's requirements and ran it through the computer. I just got the printout of boats in the area that are for sale that would satisfy his needs. It's over there. Go on, get it from that chair."

On a chaise longue twenty feet away there was a manila folder full of papers, and she walked toward it with the obedience of an unthinking robot. A plush velour robe was also draped across the chaise, and she had to lift it aside to reach the papers she needed. The robe brought back a stab of sensory memory, for it was redolent with Brett's favorite lemony after-shave cologne, and she remembered that heady smell from his closeness just the night before.

"Did you find it?"

"Yes, here it is."

"Now, if you'll look at the one I've check-marked, I think you'll see it's a good possibility."

Molly moved closer to the spa to hear him, until she noticed him looking up at her bare legs only inches from his face. She quickly sat down on a chair behind him.

"It's a 58-foot ketch, and I know the owner, he's moved to Hawaii. . . . Look, I can't keep shouting. Get in here where I can talk to you about this."

"Get in where?"

"Get in the whirlpool with me. You look as though you could use some relaxation."

"No, thank you. I don't have a swimsuit."

"Who said anything about putting on a swimsuit?" Brett laughed, and he sat up straight so that his chest rose out of the water. Molly's eyes widened at the prospect of his moving any further out of the water, for now she was sure he wasn't wearing any trunks, and she didn't require evidence to verify that verdict. She tried to concentrate on the silver medallion he wore on a chain around his neck, so that her glance wouldn't betray her fascination with the obscuring water that covered him below the waist.

"Shall I come out and meet with you there, or are you coming in here where we can talk?" Brett said with a stern threat to his voice.

"I'm sorry, but I won't go in the water without a bathing suit on," she said.

"New England girl, huh?"

"Right, New England girl."

"Rita!" Brett suddenly called out with a voice like an exultant Tarzan. "Rita, where are you?"

"I just went to make myself some breakfast, here I am," came the high-pitched reply, and from around the wall of planting bolted a beautiful young girl. She looked as though she couldn't be over seventeen years old, and she had the bright-eyed frisky manner of a palomino colt anxious to go romp in some field of clover.

"This is Molly Weston. Take her inside and give her a swimsuit. She's going to join me."

"I don't know if she could wear one of my little bitty suits," the girl said, running her fidgety fingers down her narrow waist to her boyish hips.

"There's a supply of new suits in all sizes. You know where they are."

"Oh, yes, Brett. I'll take care of it."

"Just go with Rita. She'll show you where to change, Molly."

She had been caught in her own net, and now Molly knew there was no way out of this. She'd used the lack of a suit as her only excuse, and of course Brett had found a way around her. She followed Rita to a beautiful tiled bathroom and changing area just off the patio, removed her clothing slowly, and waited for Rita to return with the promised suit.

"Here it is, this will fit," Rita said, reaching through the door to toss a bit of nylon to Molly before disappearing.

The suit was a maillot style like those used by the girls on swimming teams and it was bright purple. The size marker inside it said "6" and Molly felt a stab of panic, for while she usually wore her slacks in that size she feared there was no way she could pour herself into the size 6 bustline of this swimsuit.

Once she had it on she regarded herself in the mirror with surprised delight. She never knew she could look so sexy, with her cleavage bulging out over the plunging neckline of the suit. But she could never appear in this suit in front of Brett Sterling! Just imagining those perceiving eyes on her right now made her skin burn with embarrassment.

"Molly, are you coming out here or do I have to come and get you?" boomed Brett's voice from outside, amplified by the watery pit he was reclining in.

Molly opened the door slowly and peered about. "I'm coming. I want to get this meeting over with as badly as you do," she said as she scurried across to the row of trees. She stepped into his range of vision, and quickly turned her back to him, pretending to search for the computer printout she'd put down somewhere nearby.

"Oh, here it is," she said.

"You can't bring that into the water with you. Come here and I'll tell you all about the—"

As she turned to step quickly into the water he stopped talking mid-sentence to stare at her with an open-mouthed grin.

"Who was the fool who said that heavenly bodies only come out at night?" he said, making her more self-conscious about her voluptuous figure.

The water was so hot that it almost burned her feet and legs. She had to pause in spite of herself while she became used to the temperature. As fast as possible she worked her way down the steps and settled herself across the pool from him.

"You forgot to set the timer," he said as soon as her suit had disappeared beneath the water.

"What timer?"

"It's dangerous for a beginner to stay in a whirl-pool for over ten minutes. You're liable to get so relaxed and enjoy yourself so much that you'll forget all sense of time. Go set the timer," he said pointing to a yellow box near the chaise.

She pulled herself out from under the comfortable concealment of the water and felt Brett's eyes on her body for every one of the thirty seconds it took her to turn the dial and scamper back into the spa.

The water felt like such a hot crushing weight upon her chest that she could hardly breathe. For a long time she sat rigidly waiting to acclimatize herself. Looking across at Brett through the layer of steam rising into the cooler air above the tub, she thought he looked like an evil witch doctor who had somehow fallen into his own gurgling pot of poisons. His eyes were half-closed, his heavy upper lids casting a shadow on his wet cheeks.

Slowly she felt the muscles of her body respond to the therapy of the whirlpools that eddied around her. Every inch of her skin was being soothed by the warm touch of the jets that poured bubbles into the water.

"This doesn't seem like an atmosphere very conducive to a business meeting," she said.

"This is the very best kind of meeting. No pain, no strain, just solid comfort," he said soothingly.

"The water's hot," she complained.

"Splash some water on your face, the air will cool it. If you're still too warm, you can sit on a higher step and get your shoulders up out of the water."

She dipped water into her cupped hands and sloshed it into her face. When she opened her eyes, she noticed with horror that Brett was slowly making his way across the tub to sit beside her. Then she felt his hands under the water as he took hold of her and gently lifted her up onto the step behind her. He left one hand resting against her hip casually as he watched her obvious discomfort.

"Won't you just let go and admit you're enjoying this?" he asked. The thin purple fabric that was stretched so provocatively across her bosom was now directly at his eye level, and he made no attempt to conceal his interest as she tried to tug it into a more modest arrangement. Finally, deciding on the lesser of two evils, she lowered herself back under the water so that her swimsuit, just as his lack of one, was now safely concealed.

"The boat I have in mind is moored down at Kings Harbor. The owner has moved to Hawaii, and if you think Mr. Gunther would like to see it, I'll have Mac bring it up to my anchorage this weekend. It's a fifty-eight-foot ketch, steel hull, about thirty seven tons. It has two nice staterooms and a bunk area."

"Good stowage?"

"Yep. A very comfortable boat. You could entertain on it, party on it. I think it's just what you want."

"It's not what I want that matters."

"I kind of got the impression that you were calling the shots."

"Mr. Gunther has given me the authority to shop for him, to help him make the decision. But it's his interests I have in mind."

"How devoted you are."

"Thank you."

"Are you comfortable now?"

"Very."

"So you like the spa?"

"Yes."

"I knew you could appreciate the creature comforts."

Brett stretched one arm behind her head, nudging her head forward slightly so that he could settle his arm around her, and her head dropped back to rest on the muscles of his upper arm. Her arms and legs now felt so light that they floated, suspended in front of her. She felt the water lap at the base of her neck, and she watched with drowsy interest as the drifting currents swirled her shoulder-length auburn hair through the water around her shoulders, unconcerned that it was removing any curl she'd created this morning with her curling iron. The steam rose about her face, filling her nose, bringing a feverish feeling to her cheeks.

Molly lost all sense of time as she let the waters, and all conscious thought, stream past her body. The lethargy induced by the pool made any attempts at conversation unthinkable, and she closed her eyes and gave herself up to complete relaxation.

With his free hand Brett reached over and brushed the beads of moisture from her face. His touch awakened her as if from a drugged sleep.

"It's time," he said huskily.

"No it isn't," she answered with a detached murmur. She was not sure what schedule he was referring to, but she was sure that whatever he wanted her to do, she wasn't ready.

"You have to get out."

"But I'm just getting used to it, and the timer hasn't rung yet."

Just then she heard a sharp ping.

"You see," he said. "I have a great sense of timing. I knew your time was up."

With that he sat up straighter and placed his two hands around her waist, his strong fingers almost meeting on her back. She gave him a mindless shrug of passive resistance so that his hands slipped easily upward on the slick material of her suit until they found her breasts and he boldly caressed her. Through her torpor she fought to bring dulled senses back to life. Just last night this gesture of familiarity would have inflamed her with anger, but now she was powerless to resist him.

She gave a deep sigh, gasping to fill her lungs with cool air, and as her torso moved beneath his touch, he pushed his advantage. She lifted a lazy hand toward her face, and when she placed her palm against her cheek was surprised to find it hot to the touch. He placed one hand over hers, and with his thumb gently massaged one throbbing temple.

"You're warmed up to just the right temperature. It's really a shame to make you leave."

She was surprised to find that when she tried to

speak, her tongue felt thick and immobilized, and she slurred the words as if she were transported beyond the need for speech. "But you said I have to get out."

The hot tub had drained her of all her energy, the energy she needed to resist the seductive masculinity that Brett so enjoyed tantalizing her with. She couldn't believe how easily her body had betrayed her mind.

"Do you want me to carry you out of here?" he asked.

"No. NO! Stay where you are." She pulled away from his grasp, suddenly remembering that he probably had on nothing but the silver medal that rose and fell on his chest as he breathed.

"Let me get you a towel."

"I'll find one," she said, and yanked the strap of her suit back onto her shoulder where he had slipped it off.

She struggled to get her footing, but the pull of the water and the weakness in her legs conspired to push her where her sluggish brain was trying to tell her she should not go. She fell against his chest.

"Are you all right?" he said, gathering her close to him so that she felt the brush of the curling damp hair on his chest.

"I'm fine, really I am. You just stay right where you are. But I must get out of here."

She wondered what kind of a girl he thought she was that he would take such liberties, fondling her right out here on his patio when there were two people inside somewhere.

"Take my robe if you're cold," he said as she made her way carefully up the steps into the now-chilling breeze on the decking, clutching at the chrome safety rail for support.

"Oh, no. You'll need it. I'll be fine."

She heard a splashing sound behind her and thought with horror that he might be following her out of the pool.

"Where are you running to in such a hurry?" he called.

As she passed the chaise where his robe was resting she heard the soft thump of wet feet behind her, so she grabbed at the robe with both hands, rolled in into a bundle, and without turning around pitched it over her head straight behind her. Then she hurried as quickly as her slippery wet feet would allow toward the dressing room, hearing the taunting laughter of Brett Sterling.

"I guess the lady wants me to wear my robe," he called to no one in particular.

When Molly came out of the dressing room, she was still running her hands through her hair, exasperated that it was so thick it held the dampness even after all the toweling she had done. The cold shower she'd taken had revived her somewhat, but she still felt like Sleeping Beauty awakening from a long dream.

She saw Rita reclining on a chaise lounge nearby, brushing her long white-blond hair with impatient strokes. She was wearing a bathing suit similar to the one she'd given Molly, but the suit fit her properly, covering her lithe body fetchingly.

"Thank you for finding me a swimsuit," Molly said, more to make conversation than out of any real gratitude.

"I hope it fit OK. It was the only one I could find," the girl said with a nervous grin so brittle it looked as if it might crack her face into pieces.

Molly doubted her words very seriously, but decided to say no more about it. Brett came walking toward the girls then, wrapped and securely tied in his velour robe, Molly was glad to notice. At least she no longer had to worry about his state of undress.

"You can take the suit with you and keep it if you wish," he said.

"No thank you. I rinsed it out and hung it up to dry."

"But you wore it, or almost wore it, so well. Like a hand in a glove," he said, smiling at her with that same lascivious expression she'd seen before.

"It's not my type," she said. She began gathering up her purse and notebook, and started toward the door into the penthouse.

"See ya later," the girl called to her. She had arranged herself very comfortably and was rubbing suntan lotion all over her pale white skin as if she were quite accustomed to spending her days in Brett's office-apartment. She obviously had no official duties to interrupt her. Molly wondered just how she fit into his life, but he offered no explanation as he followed her inside.

She said, "I think the boat you've picked out sounds like a good possibility. When can Mr. Gunther see it?"

"How about this weekend?"

"I think he'd like to try it under sail."

"Then you tell him we'll take it out for a test cruise. Mac, can you go down and pick up the *Princess* tomorrow? Miss Weston would like to give her a trial run."

Mr. McKenzie was in the dining room clearing dishes off the table that Rita had apparently left untended after her late brunch.

"Sure, Miss Weston. I'll have her all ready for you."

"But, I wasn't planning to go along. It's up to Mr. Gunther, now."

Brett pinned her with a stubborn look. "Oh, but I

insist. We'll need plenty of hands to sail her over to Catalina. And besides, you've got that old man twisted around your little finger. He won't make a decision without your approval. So, you come along too."

It was more a command than an invitation so she responded in kind. "Aye, aye, sir." She knew that Brett was right, that Mr. Gunther would want her along, and with Leland's precarious health she wanted to be there to protect him from working too hard under the imperious orders of Captain Sterling.

"Be at my landing dock at six o'clock Saturday morning. Or is that too early for you?" Brett asked.

"No, that's fine. We'll be there."

"And try to find proper rigging, will you?"

"I have boat clothes," she said, hoping to sound as indignant as she felt.

When she returned home, she noticed that Mr. Gunther's car was back from the club, and she hoped he'd be having his after-lunch nap and wouldn't need her for awhile. She want to the storage area in the garages below her guest apartment, remembering that her mother had recently shipped her two trunks full of clothing and books.

When Molly first came to California, she traveled with just a few suitcases, for she wasn't sure how long she would be staying. But after a few months under Mr. Gunther's benevolent care and teaching she knew she would be here as long as he needed her. Without even being asked, Charlotte Weston had packed up the rest of Molly's belongings and sent them along to her.

"Hey, there, little girl. Is that you poking around in here?" Mr. Gunther's voice startled her.

"Were you looking for me? I can do this later if you have work for me to do," she said.

"Nah, you take your time. I just found myself too restless to take a nap. And when I heard your car come in, I hoped that meant I'd have someone to talk to." Mr. Gunther sat down with a bored sigh on the larger of the two trunks. "I'll sit right here and keep you company while you do whatever you're doing. What *are* you doing?"

"Well, it seems Mr. Brett Sterling has found you the perfect ketch, pardon my pun. And he wants to take us on a cruise this weekend to try it out. I'm just looking for my windbreaker and my heavy sweaters."

"Does it have to be this weekend? That Mr. Baxter is coming in from Chicago Friday night to take a look at my plastics plant. I'd sure like to sell that little company to him."

"We'll put Mr. Baxter up in the best hotel we can think of and tell him he can entertain himself over the weekend and then see the plant next week when it's in operation."

"That's a dandy idea. You've done it again, Miss Weston." He uncrossed his long legs and started to get up.

"Leland, you didn't wear that shirt in the Jonathan Club, I hope. The collar's all frayed and one button is loose." She stood up to go to him and she pulled at the button, easily twisting it off in her hand as proof. "See?"

He reached for her hand and held it a moment, turning his lined face up to look at her. Molly saw a bone-weariness there that frightened her.

"You see how I need you to look after me."

"I want you to bring home everything that is in your locker. I'm going to Bullocks Wilshire this afternoon and get you some new sport shirts."

Mr. Gunther clung to her hand almost pathetically as he looked across the storage room with a melancholy expression. "My dear wife, Annabelle, used to take care of all that. She managed this house, gave all my parties, saw to it that we got away for those weekends on the boat. And I was so busy I never took time to appreciate her. Until she was gone."

"You must miss her terribly."

"I do, Molly. I never realized that running all my companies and working so hard could be so lonely." His eyes were watery as he looked back to her. "You've been a real blessing to me, coming here like you did."

"I was the lucky one. When you offered me this job, I wasn't sure I could do it."

"You've done it, and you've done more. You've made me feel like I have someone in my corner again. Someone who cares what happens to me."

Molly drew her hand away from his, suddenly concerned that Mr. Gunther's unhappiness would lead him to say something rash. It had never occurred to her that he was growing dependent on her. She knew he counted on her to manage all the business details, but now for the first time she feared he was developing an emotional attachment to her. She patted his shoulder affectionately.

"You need more time to enjoy life," she said. "You must cut back on your business interests."

"I'm trying, honey. But there doesn't seem much fun in enjoying life all by myself."

She stepped carefully away from him through the odds and ends that crowded the small room. "It's not like you to feel sorry for yourself," she said with studied gentleness.

"Is that what I'm doing?"

"Yes," she said quietly, giving him a sympathetic smile to take the sting off her words.

She decided then and there that she would have to be very aware, in the days ahead, of her relationship with Leland. At his age he was facing difficult transitions, and she didn't want him to think that she could offer the solution to his loneliness.

"I guess I'd better go in and get my yachting wardrobe ready, too," he said.

"Just be at the Sterling Anchorage at six Saturday morning. Captain Bligh, or Captain Brett, will make you walk the plank if you're ten minutes late."

Molly was up and dressed by the time the sun came up on Saturday morning. She stuffed a few last-minute articles into her duffel bag and went downstairs to the garages. She was happy to see Mr. Perkins was already wiping off Leland's Cadillac.

"Do you have the directions to the dock, Mr. Perkins?"

"Oh, yes, Miss. Since you're all ready you can just take the Buick and go on down to the marina. I'll bring Mr. Gunther after he's had his breakfast. He's sure excited about this trip. I think he wants that boat real bad."

"Yes, I think it will be good for him," she agreed, and she went to her car, happy that she could drive alone and enjoy the early-morning solitude without having to make conversation all the way to the marina as Mr. Gunther would require.

The freeway swept her up into the air. She felt as if she were about to take flight through the pink-streaked clouds of the early summer morning. She drove joyously, with the same feelings of expectation she always felt before a sail.

She found the *Princess* pulled up alongside a boarding dock. It was a sleek two-masted vessel, far longer than Brett's boat, and it sported a fresh coat of bright red paint on its hull. She stood looking it over appraisingly, deciding at once that it would please her boss.

"Morning, Miss Weston," Mac called to her, waving a mop in salute. "Come aboard and stow your gear below. Yours is the aft cabin."

"Where's our captain?"

"He'll be here soon."

"Left all the dirty work for you, I see."

"By the way, you'll probably be our pot-rastler, so you'd better look over the galley and see if you have all the mess gear you'll need."

Molly had once helped crew a boat about this size in a race out of her home port, so she was not surprised by the spaciousness of the main salon. But she was impressed by the expensive attention to detail that the owner had lavished upon the boat. The design scheme was crisply nautical, with bright blue upholstered chairs, and lamps with wrapped rope bases.

A huge table dominated the midships portion with upholstered benches on each side. A book rail along each bulkhead held rows of paperback books and boxed games, so that this area was clearly the lounging and gathering place. All the way forward were two ample cabins, and toward the aft, the tiny cubicle with one narrow berth in it that had obviously been assigned to her.

After unpacking her belongings into the lockers in her cabin she checked over the galley and found that someone had filled the electric refrigerator with provisions enough to last a week. Then she went up on deck to help Mac ready the boat for the voyage. She was glad she'd worn her new blue warm-up suit, for it had plenty of stretch to the fabric so that she could bend and stoop easily as she worked.

When she heard a car pull up in the parking lot just above the dock, she stood up to look hoping that Leland had arrived. Instead she saw Brett carrying

an old duffel bag over his shoulder that was sten-
ciled, "STERLING, U.S. NAVY."

When he jumped onto the deck near her, she
noticed that he was wearing tight poplin shorts that
showed off the strength of his legs where the muscles
rounded at the calves and thighs in bulging curves.
With his oiled wool sweater and his exactly appropriate deck moccasins, he was well prepared for his
duties managing the boat.

"I see Mac's put you to work already," he said,
taking note of her flushed face and her mussed hair.
"Where's your master?"

"You mean Mr. Gunther? He's on his way. His
driver is bringing him down."

"Just in time to jump aboard for the ride but too
late to do any work, is that his plan?"

"I really hope you won't be too hard on him. He
hasn't been well and I'm hoping this trip will be
restful for him."

"I'm touched by your solicitous concern. I don't
intend to work him to death, if that's what you're
afraid of. But I'll need a lot of help setting the sails. I
hope he's an experienced seaman as you claim. I
don't need a lubber dashing around bumping into
booms all the time."

"I'm sure he'll live up to your high standards," she
said with a trace of nastiness to her voice that she
didn't try to hide.

"How about getting to the galley and making us
some coffee?" he asked her. "Mac, you have time
for a cup of java before you go ashore?" Brett
called.

"Sure, mate."

"You mean Mr. McKenzie isn't going with us?"

"He tells me he has a hot date with a shore bird
tonight so I've given him the weekend off. He
doesn't ask for that very often."

Molly cast a worried glance toward the parking lot before going below, and when she came back on deck a few moments later, a mug of hot coffee in each hand, she noticed that Brett was now doing the same thing.

"I can't understand what's keeping Mr. Gunther," she said. "He's usually so prompt." She handed the coffee to Mac and Brett.

"We have a thirty-five-mile crossing to Catalina ahead of us, and if all hands are prompt, I like to be out of the breakwater before eight o'clock," Brett said.

Just then she was relieved to see Mr. Gunther's car pulling in. She settled herself comfortably in the cockpit, sure now that nothing had gone wrong. Even without the assistance of Mac, she was sure Brett could manage the boat with Leland and her to help him. If Brett would just decide to curb his moodiness and let them all enjoy the weekend, it could be a memorable trip.

Then with a sudden pang of foreboding she noticed that Perkins was stepping gingerly down the gangplank onto the dock and heading toward her with a package in his hand. Mr. Gunther was not with him.

"Miss Weston, I have a message for you from Mr. Gunther. That Mr. Baxter called just as we were leaving. He was mad as can be at being deserted at the hotel for the weekend. Says he has to get back to Chicago on Monday and he wants Mr. Gunther to spend the weekend with him going over that plastics plant. You're to go ahead with the trip as planned. He wants you to check out the boat for him, see how it sails. And he sent this." Perkins thrust the package into her slightly shaking hands.

Molly realized that Brett was standing just above her on the boat, and was listening to the conversation without bothering to conceal his eavesdropping. She turned to look up at him and his scowl of disapproval made it clear how he felt.

"I don't know what to do," she said.

"He'll be awful disappointed, Miss Weston, if you don't do what he asks," Mr. Perkins said, and with that parting word of advice the driver turned to leave.

Molly pulled the wrappings from the gift, curious to see what Leland had sent. In the box was a new camera, with several rolls of film and a cushioned zippered case to keep the camera watertight at sea. Leland's intentions were clear. He wanted her to photograph the boat, record the journey so that he could see for himself just what it was like after she returned. And Perkins had not waited for an answer from her. Like Mr. Gunther, he expected her to do as she was instructed.

"I'm a captain without a crew," Brett said, rubbing his hands through his tousled blond hair. "First Mac has an important date and now Mr. Gunther says he's much too important to dirty his hands with rope burns."

"Now, Brett," Mac said. "Miss Weston has her sea legs. She can take her turn at the helm for you."

"That girl doesn't know port from starboard."

Molly's upper teeth bit down on her lip, so firm was her resolve to restrain the outburst she was ready to make. How like him it was to criticize her seamanship without even asking her about her experience! Her first reaction had been to cancel the trip, to tell Mr. Gunther he could do his own research or else forget about buying a boat. But now, hearing Brett's caustic dismissal, she was determined to prove to him that she could crew for him with skill and strength. She stepped onto the boat and put the camera down. Facing Brett, and the bow of the

Princess, she stretched out first her left arm and then her right.

"Port. Starboard. Any more questions, sir?"

"I suppose you taught her that, Mac."

"No sir. I got instincts when it comes to picking up scratch crews. I tell you, she knows enough to help you."

Molly appreciated Mac's endorsement, but she suspected that it was founded less on good instinct than on his desire to carry through his own plans for the weekend, and not be pushed into service by Brett. Whatever his reasons, Mac was convincing Brett.

"Do you think you can do it?" Brett turned suddenly to say to her. His direct confrontation caught her by surprise.

"I sure do."

"Well, you've got guts, I'll say that for you. Or maybe you're just foolish enough not to know what you're letting yourself in for."

"I've served under meaner captains than you before, I'm sure."

"When you serve under me, you do what I ask and you don't talk back."

"More coffee, sir?" She gave a teasing smile, which she hoped would convey her intention to keep her independence even while serving in His Majesty's service.

"No. I'm going below to listen to the weather reports."

"Looks like he's signed you on, lassie," Mac said as he gathered up the cleaning gear and prepared to abandon her to her fate.

"What can I expect out there?" she asked him, nodding her head toward the direction of the open sea. She was not used to the California waters, and she wondered if she'd been overconfident.

"Aw, it's an easy sail. It'll take six hours or so. Should be a beam reach the whole way. Keep a careful watch for tankers when you're in the shipping lanes. And don't run down any whales."

"Sounds simple enough."

Mac halted his departure long enough to place one hand on Molly's shoulder and when he looked down at her, she felt warm confidence emanating from his twinkling dark eyes. "That captain of yours seems tough as an old lanyard knot, I know. But he'll take good care of you, you'll see."

He called down the companionway, "I'm leaving now, Brett. Do you want me to take off the dock lines?"

"Yes. At least do that much for me before you hit the beach."

Brett assumed a jocular mood as he came up to put his arm around Mac, but his wincing facial expression made it clear how he dreaded the prospect of a sail with Molly. And Molly had no better attitude toward being consigned to a 58-foot floating prison with a man whose attitude toward her was so unpredictable.

"Stand by to cast off," Brett called, and Molly scurried to the cockpit to take a position behind the wheel. Brett started the engine to power out of the harbor. Then he went to work setting the sails, leaving her at the helm to guide the *Princess* through the traffic of smaller boats heading out through the jetty. With a sigh of resignation she realized they were under way.

Chapter Three

Brett had already raised the main and mizzen sails, and now that they had cleared the breakwater he raised the jib and shut off the motor. With a graceful sway the boat took the wind into her sails and began leaning into the horizon as if even an overnight mooring had been too long. No wonder boats were always referred to with feminine names, Molly thought. There was an impetuous quality to the way this boat surged forward, like a young Juliet rushing to her lover. There was no holding back, no sense of self-protection in the unleased forward movement of the *Princess*. It was up to her captain to keep her under control.

"Hold a three hundred fifty course," Brett said to Molly as he swung a watchful eye toward the compass.

It was interesting to Molly that men seemed to exhibit their true personalities in the way they sailed a boat. Some men sailed as if they were a built-in extension of the structure of the vessel. They responded to the messages of the wheel and sheets, flowing with the currents of wind and water that guided them.

Brett, on the other hand, took command of the boat beneath him, trying always to subjugate it to his own moods of rhythm and speed. As he turned the winch handle he seemed to be exerting his dominance, commanding it to tighten until it screeched with pain. At each barely discernible change in the wind he would jump into action, quick to check his control over the quaking, servile vessel under his rule. Brett Sterling, she felt sure, would never be happy with a boat over which he could not be the complete master.

But she was happy to notice that he did not extend this autocratic regime to his first mate and only crew member. Now that they had successfully brought their craft this far he seemed to relax the formality of his commands to her. Once he even smiled as he nudged her away from the wheel so that he could take over and let her rest for awhile. She found a book and stretched out on the foredeck to read, confident that he wouldn't need her now that they were set on a straight course.

She brought her nose up out of the book when she heard him call out, "Porps on the starboard!"

She looked over the side into the churning water where he was pointing and saw a gray head bob up out of the water. It was a porpoise, and as he kept ducking up and down, it appeared he was playing hide-and-seek with her in the wash of their bow. Soon she saw two more porpoises join him. With their curiously smile-shaped mouths, they seemed to consider it a happy game to swim along like Neptune's attendants at court, escorting their ship.

"I must get a picture of them. Leland will love

this," Molly said to Brett, and she found the camera bag and began fumbling with the cartons of film and the instruction booklet.

"Here, give it to me. I have a camera just like it," Brett said. As he expertly threaded the film through the notches and rollers he added, "I don't know if you realize it, but this is a very expensive camera."

"No, I didn't even think about it."

"You just accept his gifts without considering what that means?"

"I'm not sure he plans for me to keep the camera. He just wants me to take pictures of this boat for him this weekend."

"Oh, I see. A very plausible excuse. And a chance to reward you for all your cooperation."

"A gift like this doesn't mean much to Mr. Gunther."

"I would say it means a great deal."

As Brett handed the camera back to her she saw in the pale blue of his eyes a reflection of the enormous seascape around them. Those luminous orbs seemed to her bottomless, capable of holding the entire ocean in their mysterious depths. Realizing that she was staring at him, she fumbled with the camera to break her compulsion to look into those eyes.

"Have I offended you?" he asked.

"I don't know what you mean." She realized she had not been paying very close attention to his words, so fascinated was she by his close physical proximity.

"I guess you feel no guilt over what you're doing," he said. "So, how could you be offended by my criticism?"

"Oh, look. They're leaving us. The porpoises are swimming away. Now I can't get a picture."

She watched the undulating movements of the

slick and shiny sea creatures as, bored with the sport, they abandoned their game of tag with the bow of the *Princess* and swam from sight.

Molly made her way carefully out onto the bowsprit, wondering if she should snap on a lifeline. If she were to fall overboard, she wasn't too sure Brett would see the importance of turning around to pick her up. Except, of course, that he needed her two hands to help him.

She wanted to take a picture down the entire length of the boat while under sail. She leaned this way and that on the narrow metal rack over the sloshing waves that licked up to dampen her pantlegs. She had just the angle she wanted, but Brett at the wheel looked dour and forbidding.

"Could you smile?" she called to him. But apparently he couldn't hear her for he remained glum, so she took the picture in spite of him.

When she returned to his side to zip the camera back into its case, he said, "I think it's time for lunch. Let's hove to while we eat. That way we won't have to fuss with the sails. Do you want to go below and see what you can fix for us in the galley?"

Molly heated some tomato soup, poured it into large red mugs and added a sprinkling of pepper on top. Then she quickly put together some big ham and cheese sandwiches on rye bread. She took the lunch up onto the foredeck where Brett was sprawled in the sun beside a canvas drop cloth that would serve as their table.

"Lord, you've put everything you could think of into these sandwiches," he said, taking his first big bite. "Onions, tomatoes, chopped lettuce."

"Don't you like them?"

"I love them," he smiled.

She wondered why he had been so hostile toward

her just a few minutes ago. Whenever Mr. Gunther was mentioned, he seemed to descend into his most brooding mood. She couldn't figure out why he had taken such a dislike to the man.

"I know you're disappointed that Mr. Gunther didn't come along with us today," she said. "I hope you understand that something pressing came up."

"I'm not sure he's really serious about this boat project."

"Of course he is. That's why he asked me to go through with this trip in his place. Mr. Gunther never gets involved in a project unless he's planning to see it through."

"I suspect he's being influenced to do something he doesn't really want to do."

"You're right, I'm having quite a time convincing him. If he had his way, he'd work himself to death. But I think he needs a new interest, something to worry about and fuss over. I'm just hoping the boat will bring him some peace of mind."

"You are certainly trying to satisfy all his needs."

"That's what I'm paid for."

"Indeed. How true." Brett looked away from her, out across the swells that lifted them and dropped them as rhythmically as if they were sleeping in a cradle. Her lunch finished, all Molly could think about was stretching out on the warm deck and going to sleep. But Brett seemed vitalized by the meal. "It's getting very warm, don't you want to go below and change into something less cumbersome?" he asked.

"Oh, all right. I'll take all this below."

She disposed of the trash, washed out the cups, and changed into a pair of pink terry cloth shorts with a matching white trimmed top.

Brett was sitting at the navigator's table studying a big book of Catalina charts when she came out of her cabin. He stood up as she walked by, taking hold of her arm to stop her.

"Hadn't you better put on some sun cream? Your freckles are coming out like the stars at night."

"I told you, I don't give a darn," she said, as she stepped up the companionway into the sun.

The second half of the trip was smooth and effortless. By now Molly had learned to anticipate Brett's every move as he manipulated the various sail settings, testing his potency as he controlled the white billows of sail above them. No wonder he loved sailing, she thought. He needed to exert his power, to dissipate some of the temper and suppressed anger that seemed to motivate him.

Late in the day Molly became aware of a large bump on the horizon dead ahead of them. It looked like a submerged turtle through the afternoon haze, and she watched it grow steadily larger until she could be sure it was Catalina Island. Soon the small dark prickles that covered the surface of the island were transformed into trees, and she could make out the cluster of bright white buildings in one valley while the rest of the island seemed mountainous and uninhabited.

Brett was bringing down the sails and she hurried to wrap the billowing canvas neatly on the booms and tie it into place. When he went back to start up the engine, she took a seat beside him behind the wheel where she would be close enough to hear further instructions.

"I hope I have a chance to explore the island," she said.

"All seventy-five square miles of it?" Brett laughed. "We aren't going to be here that long. The back country is beautiful, very rugged and undeveloped. That's why a half-million people come over here to visit every year. It's one of the few places in

Southern California where you can turn back the clock a few years and see open land beside the sea.''

During the day they had seen only an occasional other boat, but now the traffic around them increased. Molly realized that weekend sailors were heading for their favorite destination in powerboats and sailboats of all sizes and types.

A pilot boat pulled toward them from the harbor entrance. When it drew close enough for the Harbor Patrolman on board to recognize Brett at the helm of the unfamiliar boat, he gave them a wave of greeting and sped away back to his post.

"I have my own mooring, so he doesn't need to guide me in," Brett explained. "Do you think you can handle the throttle while we tie her down?"

"I don't know. There are so many boats around! I haven't—"

"There's the buoy with my name on it. Now just guide us right between that yawl and the Chris Craft. Nice and easy, now," he called over his shoulder as he scrambled toward the foredeck.

"But which way do I push this thing?"

She noticed people sitting on deck chairs watching them with interest from surrounding boats. Apparently the favorite cocktail hour entertainment was watching how skillfully fellow seamen brought their vessels into their moorings.

Brett was now kneeling on the port bow deck, leaning toward the water reaching for the wand. She had steered them into exactly the right position, but to make it easier for him she decided to slow down a bit so they could show off and slip into their place with grace and ease.

She pushed the throttle forward and suppressing a cry of shock realized she had speeded the boat up. The bow shot past the wand. Brett scrambled to his feet and he came back toward her with a look of enraged disgust on his face.

She prepared herself for his acid critique.

"You idiot! I thought there'd be no problem bringing the boat in under power. A true sailor should be able to bring this boat into the mooring under sail and set it into place on the dime."

"And set the crowds around here cheering over their gin and tonics? Is that what you wanted?" she asked him, as she circled around the row of moored boats to make another approach.

"You go bite the waves this time." He glowered at her as he took over the wheel and pointed forward.

She took a good look at his facial expression, wondering just how vindictive the man was, and then trudged along the deck toward her watery fate, clutching at the guardwire for confidence.

Throwing herself prone upon the deck, she hung the entire upper half of her body over the side. If he were going to make a fool of her, let him do a good job of it, she decided. She wasn't going to act the least bit apprehensive.

To her relief he glided the boat to rest just as her fingers found the pick-up pole in the water. She pulled the bow hawser attached to it onto the deck and squirmed her way over to place the looped end around the cleat.

Now there was all the tying down to finish and she followed Brett from fore to aft finding ways to be of assistance, wishing he would acknowledge that she had performed at least some part of her duties well. At last he uttered the compliment she had been waiting for.

"At least you didn't get seasick."

"Did you expect me to?"

"I always carry some pills just in case."

"It's never happened to me, even in a sea full of swells like today."

"Well, maybe there's hope for you, yet," he said.

It wasn't much, but it was better than "you idiot," she decided.

"Should I go to the galley and fix supper?"

"It's an old Avalon custom. We have a nice quiet Happy Hour, and then the captain broils the steaks and tosses the salad."

"Oh really? I like that old custom."

She watched him for awhile as he attached a stainless steel barbecue to one of the stanchions, lit the charcoal, and swung it out over the water. Then she decided to go below and clean up.

Anticipating a cool evening ahead, Molly slipped into an ankle-length sweatshirt dress with a hood. It had a soft fleece lining that felt good against her sun-polished skin. No makeup in the world could camouflage the freckles she'd sprouted during the hours in the sun, so she wore none, simply rubbed some sweet smelling lotion onto her cheeks to add to their glow. She brushed at her hair for a long time to remove the effects of the salty spray, then combed it into a thick straight tress down her back.

When she emerged topside, Brett was sitting with a drink in his hand, staring at the shimmering waters of Avalon, painted with the red and gold colors of the sunset.

"You mentioned a gin and tonic so that's what I made for you," he said, indicating a fresh drink waiting for her. He'd brought two stereo speakers up from the main cabin and he'd tuned in an FM station.

"Now that you're as clean as a new penny, I think I'll go get cleaned up, too," Brett said, patting her coppery hair as he stepped past her.

She picked up the book she had left on deck, content to be alone for the next half hour.

"Do you always have your nose in a book? How can you ignore a beautiful setting like this to sit in the half-dark and read?"

Molly looked up with a startled expression to realize the sun had set and that the twilight sky was darkening.

Brett had changed into a pair of chocolate brown corduroy pants. He wore a creamy white sweater complementing the deep tan of his face.

"Say, pick up that book again. I think there's enough light left." He reached for her camera bag and took out the new camera.

"Stay just the way you are, with your legs curled up under you. That's it, now hold the book in one hand, and lean your other hand on the lazaret."

She imitated the pose he had found her in a moment ago when he'd chided her for her reading. He quickly adjusted all the camera settings and clicked off several pictures.

"That sky behind you is beautiful. It should make a very fetching photograph. Your Mr. Gunther will love it. He'll probably have it blown up to life-size and hang it over his desk."

"I doubt that. And could we get off the subject of Mr. Gunther? It only seems to irritate you."

"You've noticed."

"Of course I have."

"There are things I'd rather discuss," he said, sitting down beside her. "The *Princess* for instance."

"She's a beautiful boat."

"And we're here together alone, just the three of us, you, me and the *Princess*."

Molly looked around her. The decks of the boats nearby were empty. Most people had gone below to eat dinner. She could hear the muted sounds of laughter and clinking dinnerware over the soft throb of the stereo music. In spite of the crowd of boats around them, she felt quite alone with Brett. The water encircled them like a moat.

Brett was watching her. In spite of the twilight, she could see he was smiling.

"So this is Happy Hour," she said with a long, contented sigh.

"Yes, and are you happy?"

"I'm always happy when I'm on board a trim vessel like this one. I can tell you feel the same way."

"You're right. If I had my way, I'd spend every day just like this one, under full sail with a balmy sky overhead. Having a pretty girl on board lifts my spirits too," he said.

Molly picked up her drink, and took a long sip to her dry mouth. "I suppose your business interests keep you too busy to spend much time with sailing," she said.

"I make sure I have time for the pleasures of life, believe me."

She did believe him. What she wondered was how he ever found the time to manage his vast holdings of marina property, so intent did he appear to be at pursuing his hedonistic diversions. A question popped out of her mouth before she could stop it.

"That girl I met at your place, Rita?"

"What about her?"

"Does she like to sail?"

"Loves it. She's rather new at it, but she's an eager pupil."

I'll just bet, thought Molly.

Brett stood up, apparently in an effort to change the course of the conversation. "I'll go get the meat, I think that fire's about ready."

"Is there anything I can do?"

"The table's all set, the salad is ready to toss. You can warm up some French bread if you like."

It was very pleasant working in tandem with him this way, just as they had all day long. She hummed softly along with the music as she worked. By now she was familiar with the galley and she had everything ready by the time Brett brought the cooked steaks down.

"We have to conserve power," he said, turning off the battery-powered cabin lights, and he brought a candle in a hurricane holder to the table and lit it. "Besides, this is more romantic."

As they ate their dinner Molly felt the effects of that romantic atmosphere. She felt sheltered and cozy sharing the snug dining alcove with him, watching the constant motion of the candle flame as it played across the polished surface of the table and the burnished planes of his face. Sitting across from her, Brett often stopped eating to sit back and sip some wine and regard her with a contagious smile of satisfaction. Molly couldn't help but smile back at him.

"Won't you have some more wine? It will warm the cockles of your heart."

"My cockles don't need it, they're quite warm enough, thank you," she said, already feeling the lulling effects upon her of a day in the sun.

"Is that so?" he said, lowering his eyes so that the shadows above his head crept down his high cheekbones, giving him a mysterious, masked appearance. "The warmer the better," he said, topping off her wine glass in spite of her protest.

At that point, Molly began to feel a mounting apprehension. Like a cold wet wave of seawater, a tide of angry fear rose slowly up from her toes until she felt chilled all over. She found herself breathing fast in shallow gasps of panic. She looked around the cabin, suddenly feeling isolated, alone with Brett's obvious expectations.

Were they both to spend the night here on the boat? Brett had said nothing about finding her a hotel room at Avalon, and it was already nine o'clock. What would the people on the neighboring boats think if she spent the night with him alone on the *Princess?* Brett, no doubt, used this mooring for romantic interludes with a variety of companions. His neighboring yachtsmen would no doubt consider her just one more in a string of boat groupies who came for weekend fun with the irresistible Brett Sterling. But how did Brett himself view the weekend? Plying her with wine and talking of the romantic atmosphere, he obviously didn't plan to spend the long night ahead of them alone in the captain's stateroom while she finished her book in her cabin.

"What's the matter, Molly? You aren't touching your food," Brett said. "A day at sea is supposed to make your appetite ravenous."

"I have no appetite at all. I think I need some air. It's stuffy down here. Go ahead and finish your dinner."

"I'm through. I'll just put things shipshape again and come out and join you on deck."

Molly stumbled up the companionway ladder into the dark cockpit. During the short time she'd been below the weather had changed. A layer of low clouds floated in front of the moon. A chilly breeze grasped at her.

How could I have been so stupid? Molly thought. *I should have headed off this situation hours ago. I know what kind of man Brett is. How accustomed he is to having his own way. I should have known he would consider it his obligation to romance me. Now I have to let him know at once how I feel.*

She curled up miserably on a cushion, thrusting

her hands into the deep fleece handwarmer pockets of her dress. She didn't look forward to another unpleasant scene with the demanding man. She heard Brett coming, whistling to the music. She noticed that the stereo had been changed to a soft-rock station. The music throbbed sensuously through the night air, just loud enough to cover the sound of their voices—*so that no one can overhear,* Molly thought.

"How anyone could get claustrophobia on a boat this size, I don't know," Brett said. "But what's the difference? We'll spend the night out here under the stars." He sprawled beside her.

"There are no stars. There's a cloud cover."

"I see two stars," he said turning to regard her carefully. "And they're shining brightly enough for a navigator to steer his ship by. You have eyes like lodestars, Molly. A man could follow them right off the edge of the earth."

"I have a news flash for you. Columbus has proved the earth is round." She cuddled down into her warm dress, shivering.

Brett seemed to take her gesture as an invitation to put his arms around her. "Now, isn't this better?" he asked in a husky voice.

"Brett, there's something you have to understand about me."

"I understand all about you."

He wrapped his arms so tightly about her that her face was brought directly beneath his. She could feel his breath on her cheeks in short gusts that were as warming as his embrace. Her lips parted involuntarily as he moved his mouth to press it against hers in a thrilling, exploratory kiss. She felt as if she were an obstinate *Princess* trying to sail against the wind, tilting dangerously, and that her captain was intent upon slowing her down, spilling some of the wind from her sails, so that they would shiver under his control.

She knew, as she gave herself up to the complete enjoyment of his lips, that she had only one enemy on board this vessel. That enemy was her own traitorous body. In spite of herself, her hands came out of her pockets to caress the soft wool sweater where it stretched over Brett's huge shoulders as she matched his ardor.

"I'm sure you won't find it so stuffy below decks now," he whispered in her ear when she at last drew herself away from his kiss.

"I want to go to my cabin," she stammered.

"Your cabin is scarcely big enough for one," he laughed softly. "Let's give that master stateroom a trial run."

"You don't understand—"

Brett pulled the hood of her dress up around her hair, holding the soft fabric in his hands on each side of her face, and using it to pull her toward him for two quick, soft kisses. "You're getting too cold out here, baby. Come with me."

His words gave her a glow of anticipation that she was quick to stifle. How many other girls had heard this same invitation? How many times did this heartless playboy think he could repeat his winning ploys?

"I don't want to go to your cabin with you, and I want you to leave me alone!" she said hotly, moving away from his reach to sit on the other side of the cockpit.

"What's the matter with you? Do you think it's more exciting to resist? If you are trying to build the suspense, forget it. I'm ready for you. I want you right now." He leaned across to take her hands into his, and he looked into her eyes in a way that was so appealing that she almost forgot her protest.

"You've made a terrible mistake. You don't know me, you don't know what kind of a girl I am."

"I know exactly what kind of a girl you are. So don't play the innocent. Why not cooperate and make this little business junket of ours more pleasant for both of us?"

She pulled her hands away. "I am not going to cooperate, as you call it."

"Stop playing the tease. It doesn't suit you."

"I'm not trying to tease you. When you kissed me, I didn't mean to encourage you."

"Encourage me!" He jumped up with a charging motion too big for the space, and she feared he would throw anything overboard that got in his way. "You tormented me, that's what you did."

"I'm sorry. Why do you expect every girl you meet to give in to you?"

"I don't want every girl I meet. I want you."

"Well, you can't have me. I want to go to my cabin alone. No more romantic games."

Brett leaned against the hatch cover blocking her way to the steps and stared sullenly into the darkness. Then he said with malicious, even words, "I think I get the picture now. You've signed yourself up to some kind of exclusive contract."

"What do you mean?"

"Mr. Leland Gunther has obviously bought you, body and soul."

"Why, what are you talking about. Leland is my—"

"Oh, it's 'Leland' now, is it? What happened to the 'Mr. Gunther' you were always so careful to say when you were playing the efficient little executive secretary?"

"I *am* his secretary."

"Don't kid me. You're much more than that. You live at his house, you drive his cars, he gives you expensive gifts, you pick out his playthings for him. You've got that man running fore and aft for you. I should have known you wouldn't want to jeopardize a deal like that by spreading your favors around."

"Do you realize what you're saying? Why, no one has ever questioned my relationship with my employer."

"I'm sure you've played the role of a very proper employee. But I could see through it the first time I kissed you. By your car at the marina, if you remember."

"Let me by," she said, standing up quickly. Tears of humiliation were blurring her sight as she made her way to her tiny cubicle and slammed the door shut.

The aft cabin was so small that there was only a narrow strip of floorspace. Kneeling on top of the berth, she stripped off her dress and changed into her nightgown. Slipping into bed, she turned out the light. As she lay in the dark she could hear the boat creak and feel its sway. She thought she heard Brett stalking about restlessly on the decks over her head.

She must have gone to sleep immediately. But in a few hours the turmoil that churned even her sleeping mind awakened her. She heard the nautical clock in the main salon chime three o'clock and she turned on the reading light just above her head. Even tied as securely as it was to the concrete blocks on the harbor bottom, the boat was swaying and rocking back and forth. Apparently a wind storm had come up while she slept, for she could hear halyards whipping about against the masts, and metal guy wires humming.

She picked up a book and tried to read, but ugly words in her memory crowded out comprehension of the words in front of her. How could Brett have said those things? How could he believe that she was

Leland Gunther's mistress? And now that he believed it, how could she ever convince such a stubborn man that his censure was unfounded?

She tried to force her thoughts to the more pleasant moments of the evening before. Before she could understand why, she was crying. Perhaps the tears started as she replayed Brett's compliments over cocktails, or his look across the dinner table. He could be such a tremendously appealing person when he wanted to be! His touch could be so gentle, his lips so searching, his eyes so many fathoms deep! With each memory of the bewitching sensations offered by Brett Sterling, more tears flowed. She was unquestionably attracted to him, she responded to his touch in spite of all her resolve to resist him. And yet he had cast a stone at her which was so wounding she doubted she would ever recover from the shame of it.

Molly's increasing frustration as she considered her infuriating predicament was matched by the increasing motion of the boat. The *Princess* was pitching and rolling as if she wanted to leap from the ropes that tied her to the mooring and run off to follow wherever the zesty winds would lead her. Molly got up onto her knees to peek out through her porthole. She saw the boats nearby tipping their masts to one another in worried conversation.

She felt like a prisoner below decks where every pitch and yaw seemed menacing. Though she knew her fear was unreasonable, she had a horrible vision of the boat tipping over with her trapped beneath it. If only she could be outside, she knew she would feel more confident.

For warmth, she pulled the sweatshirt dress on over her nightgown and cautiously opened the thin door to her cabin, which had been rattling on its hinges in response to the winds. The main salon was dark, but she could make out the closed door of the master cabin. She didn't want to awaken Brett. Using the light from her cabin to guide her, she headed toward the steps and slowly slid back the hatch.

Brett had put up the canvas canopy over the cockpit so that it was now a rather protected place where she could curl up on watch and keep her trained weather eye on the rapidly changing conditions. She snuggled into the cushions and tried to concentrate on the soothing motion as the boat swayed. She tipped her head back and closed her eyes, but her heart still pounded as heavily as the waves upon the dock across the way. Now and then a gust of wind whipped around a corner of the canvas to whirl her hair.

It was too dark for her to notice right away the lump of sleeping bag that was spread out on the foredeck, or to notice that the shape was moving. But she did notice when Brett pulled himself out of the sleeping bag and came back to join her in the cockpit. Her eyes flew open as he slipped into place beside her. He put his arm around her and drew her close to him, spreading the sleeping bag over them like a warm blanket.

"Don't jump like that. You have no reason to be afraid of me," he said, in a strangely controlled voice.

She didn't want to tell him that it was her own attraction to him that frightened her.

"I'm not planning to attack you. I just want to share your warmth," he said.

"I came up to check on things," she said haltingly.

"Didn't you know I'd be on nightwatch during a windstorm like this?" he asked.

"Well, I—"

"You were frightened, weren't you? Why don't you admit it?"

"I guess I was. I feel better out here where I can—"

"Just relax and trust the *Princess*. She can weather anything. There's no reason to be afraid. When you're up against a situation you can't fight, then you have to give up and sit it out."

She looked at him covertly, but in the darkness she could only see the flash of his white teeth against the shadows of his face. She hoped that he meant he was not going to force himself on her anymore.

Brett was so close to her that she was overpowered by the musky masculine fragrance emanating from his sleeping bag. She leaned against him heavily, for she was not afraid of the storm here on the topside and his presence was so undemanding now that she could enjoy having him near. His arm about her shoulders held her tightly so that her motions became a part of his. They both moved in concert with the *Princess*, and with the wave action of the harbor waters.

Maybe the winds were now playing themselves out, for the disquieting gusts of just a few moments before seemed slowed, and her heartbeat returned to normal. She had never imagined that Brett could have such a comforting influence over her; their contacts had always been so full of friction. She felt protected and secure in his arms, and she let the tiring emotions of the day take their toll on her as she fell into a restful half-sleep.

She was almost disappointed when she awakened to find that she was alone in the damp cockpit. The glow of morning light had roused her. As she sat up and looked around her, she realized that the sun was filtering through a layer of fog so thick that it was impossible to see the source of the light. The sea was calm. It was so quiet that Molly was unnerved by the feeling of suspended animation. She knew that Brett was somewhere nearby and she knew there were boats moored only a few yards away, but the curtain of fog that had descended around the boat gave her the lonely feeling of being wrapped in sound-baffling bunting.

Brett was wide-awake as he hurried by her. "The radar seems to be broken. It doesn't pick up anything. So don't hurry to report for duty; we aren't going anywhere in this pea soup."

"Good morning to you, too," she mumbled under her breath, as he disappeared below decks too intent upon his repair project to hear her.

She pushed the sleeping bag aside, grateful that at least Brett had arranged it over her in such a way that she had been protected from the dew-laden night air. Everything around her was wet with a layer of mist.

As she struggled to come awake and get to her cabin to dress she realized that the fog might cut them off from the outside world for quite some time. If the radar were indeed broken, they couldn't leave here until the visibility had improved.

How could she stay on this boat with him indefinitely? Just the two of them alone together in this small space all day and, worse yet, probably another night. They would be sure to reopen their terrible argument. She knew he would repeat the reprehensible accusation and that she was powerless to defend herself. He considered her the plaything of a wealthy man. She couldn't bear to hear him say it again.

She put on warm slacks and a sweater and stuffed the rest of her things into her duffel bag. She had seen a rubber dinghy lashed to the foredeck, and if she could get to it while he was occupied with the troublesome radar equipment, she could get away from him.

She slipped across the wet decks to the foredeck, threw her duffel into the dinghy, and began untying the cumbersome knots. A foghorn boomed out its sad call from somewhere nearby; the sound reverberated in the heavy air. If Brett caught her, he would be furious. She worked at the ropes with trembling fingers.

At last she was ready to lower the dinghy over the side. It made a heavy thud as it hit the water, but the sounds of Brett working below continued, so she assumed he was too preoccupied to have heard it. Stepping over the side into the bobbing boat, she grasped the oars.

Molly could just make out the dim shape of the neighboring yacht. She started off in that direction. From there she would sight another, and then another, and make her way to the dinghy dock. But once she was alone in the vulnerable little rubber boat she wondered if it had been wise to let Brett's threat to her composure force her into what could become an even more threatening adventure.

Chapter Four

Molly rowed expertly, with arms that were strengthened by her resolve to get away from the temptations that Brett Sterling set whirling through her crazed mind. She shivered in the cold, remembering the warmth of the sleeping bag and Brett's body beside hers during the night. But she would be safer away from him, she promised herself with each stroke of the oars.

She passed one boat after another, and within a few minutes she sighted the bright green pier and the dinghy dock where she could tie up her boat and leave it for Brett to find later.

Just as she was slipping her dinghy in between the others that were crowded into place while their owners were onshore, she heard the loud blast of an airhorn from somewhere in the bay. That was the sound of someone summoning a shoreboat and she assumed that Brett had already discovered her absence and was coming after her. She hurried to tie his dinghy securely, grabbed her duffel bag, and hurried up the ramp onto the pier. If the shoreboat answered his call promptly, he would be close behind her, and she looked around her with confusion wondering where she could go to avoid him.

She left the pier and hurried down the wide brick sidewalk beside the water that served as the main pedestrian thoroughfare of Avalon, facing restaurants, shops and hotels. When she reached the first side street where auto traffic was allowed, she paused before crossing, and an opensided van pulled up right in front of her and began unloading passengers. The vehicle said Zane Grey Hotel on the side and the friendly young man behind the wheel noticed her interest and leaned across to call to her.

"Were you looking for a ride up the hill to our place?"

"Maybe so. Do you have any vacancies?"

"Sure do. Hop aboard."

"Where is your hotel?"

"See the clock tower up there on the hill? We're that old pueblo just to the left. It used to be Zane Grey's home. Wait until you see the view from his front porch."

She looked up between drifting patches of fog to see the old home that had once belonged to the famous writer of western novels. Brett would never think to look for her way up there; he'd check the hotels on the main streets first, she was sure of that.

As soon as she was shown to her room at the hotel she went to the window. She could see every boat moored in the harbor below and she had no trouble picking out the *Princess* with its bright red hull. There was no sign of Brett on the boat but now that the fog was clearing she hoped he had given up his pursuit of her. Maybe he was at this moment below decks, preparing to sail home without her.

Restlessly she stalked her small room, unpacking a few things, trying to decide what to do next. She couldn't hide here like a fugitive all day, she decided. She wrapped a blue scarf over her head and knotted it at the back of her neck so it would hide her bright hair. Then, with some dark glasses on as a further disguise, she decided it was safe to walk down into town and see a bit of Catalina as she had wanted to do.

She was just beginning to enjoy the bustling vacation atmosphere of the town of Avalon when she stopped suddenly in her tracks. She spotted Brett Sterling about fifty feet away from her. He was looking into a shop window, probably trying to see if she was inside. He must have seen someone who resembled her for he stepped into the shop, and Molly knew she only had a few moment's grace in which to get away from him.

She turned around and rushed back to the corner she'd just passed. There a man behind a counter was renting jeeps for people who wanted to explore the hills around Avalon, and she rushed over to him with her wallet already open. He gave her a special map, with a suggested route indicated. She jammed it into her purse and asked which vehicle she was to take.

"Do you want one with the top up, or the top down?" he asked.

"It doesn't matter. I'll just take this one right here with the top down," she said.

"Are you used to driving a stick shift?"

"Yes, yes. I'm sure I'll have no trouble."

After a couple of disappointing cold turnovers the engine started. She saw Brett emerge from the shop down the way. He was heading toward her and when she saw his step quicken, she knew that he had seen her. The jeep with its unfamiliar gear box jumped like a startled horse before taking the bit and pulling her steadily up the road away from Brett. At the first stop sign Molly turned around in her seat to squint back down the street, and she saw Brett standing directly in front of the rental desk watching her.

She sped through the narrow streets of the town toward the Pebbly Beach Road that led along the water and then wound up toward Mt. Ida. She throttled the lurching vehicle up the serpentine curves. Eucalyptus trees lined the edges of the road, then there was a steep drop-off to the water below, but she was too involved in the race to take notice of the beautiful view. She guessed that Brett would rent a jeep and follow her, and he would know she was taking the mapped route. She had to stay ahead of him if she were to avoid him.

She passed the entrance to the majestic Wrigley estate and kept right on going, and eventually the road curved down again into a confusing narrow valley full of new condominiums. She had to stop a moment to consult the map. Rather than returning to town, she decided to take the long road up the mouth of Avalon Canyon. It led to a botanical garden where she hoped there would be enough tourists for her to get lost in.

As she sped past the stables and the golf course, she heard the sound of another jeep behind her and she knew that Brett was narrowing in on the chase. There were no paved side roads, there was no place to escape, so she sped on, the wind tugging her hair out from under the scarf.

When she reached a parking lot at the road's end in the top of the canyon, she pulled behind some trees and ran toward the turnstile entrance to the botanical garden. She could see that once she was inside there were curving paths where she could disappear amongst the samples of native California trees and shrubs.

She immediately detoured off the main path onto a narrow gravel walk into a cactus garden. She bent low, pretending to examine the name plates before each specimen so that she would be shielded from the view of anyone coming up the main path. From various parts of the garden she could hear the voices of visitors, but this particular area seemed deserted and she congratulated herself on her clever strategy in somehow losing her pursuer. She knew she might have to stay here for awhile, but the day was lovely and the surroundings bucolic. If only she could find a bench, she would sit down and try to enjoy the calm relief of having evaded Brett.

Around the next bend in the walk there was indeed a bench, and seated on it, leaning back with his right ankle resting comfortably upon his left knee, was Brett Sterling, looking nothing like a villainous tracker. To emphasize his lack of effort in having trapped her, he flicked an imaginary speck from his spotless white sweatshirt, pulled a nonexistent thread from his matching white duck pants, and then regarded her with no trace of the irritation he must be feeling.

"Enjoying your tour of the island?"

Molly looked down the path in both directions, realizing that trying to make a run for it was pointless. He had obviously seen her go into the cactus garden and he'd merely gone farther up the main walkway and found the other end of her path and met her on it halfway.

Since avoidance was impossible, Molly decided she must try to appear unperturbed. She sat down on the bench beside him as if she had no care in the world. Perhaps if she looked serene on the outside, the feeling would soon come to her.

"I'm sorry I left this morning without saying good-bye. I just decided I wanted to see a bit of the island," she said.

"How about walking on up to the Memorial?" He stood up and gestured toward the top of the canyon where there was an imposing structure with wide circular staircases and a tall white tower.

"I thought I'd do that, yes."

"But you don't require any company, is that it?"

"I'm sure you have other things to do on the boat."

"It's too late to return to the mainland. I thought we could leave first thing tomorrow morning."

"I've checked into a hotel. I'll spend the night there."

"You weren't comfortable on the *Princess?*"

"No."

"You seemed to sleep comfortably enough last night."

Molly stood up, and backed away from him almost without being aware she was doing so. She was shaken by the memory of how easily she had fallen asleep in his arms last night, how warm and safe it had seemed to spend the night beside him. But by this morning's bright light he seemed anything but comforting.

"I did not like staying alone on the boat with you. I don't think it looks right."

"You sure have confused notions about propriety."

"I care very much about what people think. Is it so hard for you to believe that my reputation matters to me?"

"No, I realize you pay a lot of attention to putting up a good front."

"It's not a front," she said, feeling the anger rising up in her again. Brett had moved threateningly close to her, and she felt trapped by the constricting pressure of his constant innuendos.

"Look out! You're right between a Red Hot Poker and a Spanish Dagger," Brett said.

Molly looked around, wondering what he meant.

"Those cacti on each side of you: one's a Yucca called the Spanish Dagger, or the Spanish Bayonet. And that sharp thing on the other side of you is aptly named the Red Hot Poker. And if you jump any further away from me, you'll land in the Prickly Pear."

Molly realized that Brett had again backed her into a corner. He had carefully maneuvered her off the walkway and right between two menacing cactus plants. He towered over her, his huge shoulders blocking out the sun behind him so that she felt she was cowering in the shadows.

"Now you're in no position to make pious proclamations, are you?" he said. "So, I'll make all the deals, is that understood?"

She nodded, her elbow painfully brushed by the spear of the plant that crowded at her left side.

"You go ahead and do your island touring, but I want you to meet me at six o'clock for an early dinner, and then you'll have some deckhand duties to perform to get the boat ready."

She pulled her eyes away from his riveting look and studied her feet noncommittally.

"You show up for dinner at the Upstairs, it's right on the main street, and I'll let you spend the night respectably ensconced at your hotel. But if you don't appear at six o'clock, I'm coming to get you."

He walked over to the bench where he'd been

sitting and now she noticed her camera bag, which he'd brought with him.

"I really only came to bring you this. I was sure you'd want to use your new toy while you're touring about. Here."

He tossed the camera bag to her with a sudden hard pitch. When she caught it, the force of it pushed her backward so that both arms received the painful brush of the cacti. But now that he had turned to walk away from her she was able to free herself from her spiny cage, and she stepped back into the sunshine and freedom of the open walkways.

Molly stood for a moment, watching Brett's head over the tall planting, to make sure he was leaving. She could follow the familiar mop of blond curls all the way to the main path, and assured herself he was heading toward the entrance gate and his parked jeep. She had lost her interest in seeing the rest of the gardens, and before long she was walking back between the Catalina Cherries and the red-berried toyon trees to the parking lot.

After returning the jeep she wandered into the Tourist Center nearby and the girl behind the counter gave her an enthusiastic description of the Glass Bottom Boat tour that would be leaving the dock shortly. But Molly had too many emotional memories of her recent boat trip, and decided instead to return to her hotel for a calming swim in the pool.

The pool water was cold, but it felt good to her, and she was happy to have the pool all to herself for the next half hour. After the chilling swim she went back to her room and got into bed to warm herself and take a short nap.

The clock tower was only a short distance away from Mr. Grey's pueblo, and she awakened some time later to hear its melody chiming over the town to announce the time. It was a quarter to six already, and she had to dress and walk all the way down the hill to find the restaurant where Brett had ordered her to meet him. He probably already had a lobster in front of him, his own claws bared, ready to do battle with the spiny little monster. Brett had set the dinner hour early, forsaking his beloved Happy Hour so that he could put her to work on the boat as soon as possible.

Since she would be working later in the evening she pulled on her stretch denim jeans, but since they were going to eat out she wore with them a new ruby-red pullover of soft velour. She arranged her hair hastily, brushing it over her free hand so that it curved under slightly all the way around.

As she dashed lipstick across her mouth she tried to think if there was anything she could do to improve her appearance. She remembered some small gold hoop earrings she'd brought along, and squandered a minute more of her precious time to fasten them at her ears. That would have to do, she sighed as she leaned forward to look at herself in the mirror. The ruby shirt was bringing out the red highlights in her hair and her tan almost blended her freckles into one another, so the total effect satisfied her critical eye. She grabbed her windbreaker and hurried out the door.

When she found the Upstairs Restaurant, she stood on the sidewalk a moment and looked up at the tables beside the windows, looking for Brett as she paused to catch her breath. The chimes, fainter now than when they had awakened her outside her window just fifteen moments ago, began to sound the hour.

"You're right on time, I see." She heard Brett's voice behind her, and turned to see him ambling across the brick promenade from the seawall where he'd been sitting. "I guess you took my threat seriously. You didn't want me to come and drag you from wherever you were hiding. Where were you, by the way?"

"I was in bed."

"In *bed?*" he laughed heartily, enjoying the discomfort that burned her cheeks. "Now I wish I had come after you."

"I mean, I'm staying at the Zane Grey. That's where I was."

"I know you were in bed. I can still see the bloom of sleep on your cheeks. Shall we take a short stroll and see if we can rouse you?"

"I thought you wanted to eat right away."

"There's no hurry. Come on, the walk out to the casino is beautiful," he said, and, without waiting for her agreement, he started off.

When he saw that she was hesitating, he took her by the arm to lead her, maintaining a firm hold as they fell into step together. The boardwalk was lined with palm trees, and their fronds vibrated in the sea breeze like grass skirts at the hips of native dancers.

At the very tip of the harbor promontory stood the round white Grand Casino that looked like a twelve-story wedding cake. They walked all the way around it, and then Brett helped her up onto the rocks of the breakwater that extended out into the sea to modulate the surges of storms.

"Watch your step," he cautioned, and he insisted on holding her hand and helping her from rock to rock. One slip and she would slide down the rocks into the dark black water already shaded from the setting sun by the surrounding hills.

When they reached a large flat rock almost at the end of the jetty, he sat down and indicated with a pat on the rock beside him that he expected her to sit beside him. Then he drew from the pockets of his jacket a pipe and a bag of tobacco.

"I didn't know you smoked a pipe," she said.

"Mac gave it to me. He says it is supposed to be a soothing habit. Good for the disposition."

She was glad to see that he recognized the abrasiveness of his own personality and was trying, at least at the moment, to suppress some of that antagonism.

She watched him as he ignited a long flame from a pipe-lighter, and sat puffing the tobacco to life. Then, when he had put the lighter away and had one hand free, he used it to take her hand into his.

The sweet, rosy smell of the tobacco was pleasant, and the pipe seemed to have the soothing effect Mac had promised, for they sat together wordlessly, enjoying the evening from their secluded vantage point. They watched a cabin cruiser chug into the harbor at the end of its channel crossing, the wake behind it forming a V that almost filled the sea to the horizon. Across on the opposite side of the harbor they saw day visitors filing onto the 700-passenger cruiser that would take them on its regular run back to the mainland, sunburned, windblown and invigorated.

When the clock chimed seven, she was surprised to realize how long they had spent together so painlessly. He put the pipe away, and they began a leisurely paced walk back along the palm trees, now lighted from below so that they seemed even taller and more dramatic than before.

Of course, Brett Sterling had no trouble capturing one of the best tables near a window of the restaurant, and of course, just as Molly had predicted, he ordered lobster. She decided to try the abalone almandine, and while waiting for their fish, they enjoyed a thick white clam chowder.

His soup consumed, Brett pushed the empty bowl to one side, leaned both elbows on the table, and rested his chin on his hands. Then he regarded Molly with a searching look.

Finally he said, "Here on this island I feel a million miles from reality, a long way from all the problems at home."

"Do you have problems waiting for you?"

"Of course, don't you?"

"Not particularly." Molly felt that all her problems would be over once she was free of the overwhelming presence of Brett Sterling.

"I feel as if I don't want to go back. Everything I hate and despise will be waiting there for us," he said, looking away from her toward the window so that she couldn't see his facial expression.

"Well then, while you're here why don't you put all thoughts of the mainland out of your mind?" she suggested.

"I've been trying to do that. But there are constant reminders."

Molly understood that Brett's extensive business holdings probably forced him to devote more of his mental energy to his work than he cared to. And apparently, some business problems were now troubling him so that he could not enjoy his leisure hours. But she couldn't help the guilty feeling he was giving her that somehow she was responsible for his worries. Did the sale of this one boat mean so much to him? Was he angry because he had wasted his weekend on demonstrating the boat to her when it was Mr. Gunther he needed to impress?

"I'm sorry if this weekend has been a disappointment to you," she said.

"A disappointment? Do you think I'm sitting here crying crocodile tears of self-pity because of what happened last night?"

That was not what Molly had meant at all, and she was startled by the vehemence of his denial. Certainly her rejection couldn't have meant much to him, he had such little regard for her.

She spoke tentatively. "I just meant that you were disappointed because Mr. Gunther didn't come on this trip."

"I'm not the least bit upset by his absence. I'm only sorry I have to do business with him at all."

The waitress came at that opportune moment to serve their dinners, and they both turned their attention to the seafood, glad to avoid any further discussion of the unpleasant topic that always seemed to erupt between them. It was clear that Brett had the worst possible opinion of Mr. Gunther, and of Molly as well because of the association with him that he presumed she had. And he could not resist the temptation to remind her at every opportunity of how he felt.

While they finished their dinner they exchanged weather predictions and comments on other safe topics until Molly was sure there would be no more mention of his antagonisms, and they could coexist without the flareups that so upset her. But she was quite wrong, for Brett had saved his most important news for last.

After he paid the waitress and they sat waiting for his change she asked him what they had to do tonight to ready the boat for departure tomorrow.

"I'm afraid our schedule has been changed. We're leaving tonight."

"Is that possible?"

"The radar has been fixed, and a night sail in clear weather is no problem."

"But why can't we wait until morning?" Molly did not relish the idea of setting out tonight after the unstable weather conditions that had caused such abrupt changes every few hours for the past day or so.

"Because you have received a summons from your very demanding keeper. And as I have already learned, when Mr. Gunther speaks, you jump."

"Have you heard from Mr. Gunther?"

"Yes. By radiophone this afternoon. He finds that he has a few hours tomorrow morning to inspect the *Princess,* and he wants her docked and ready for him at the marina. That means we'll have to shove off in an hour or so in order to meet his exact schedule."

"I wish I had talked to him. Perhaps I could have convinced him that we should wait until tomorrow to sail back."

"I'm sure your talents for convincing him would have been more persuasive than mine. But, unfortunately, you were not available to wheedle him into seeing it your way."

"I'm sure he could arrange to see the boat another time."

"That was not his only reason for telling me to return immediately. He also had a message for you."

"What was it?"

"He said to tell you that he has a big surprise for you, and that you must be back to receive it tomorrow."

"What kind of surprise?"

"He didn't say, but knowing his generosity toward you, you can probably make some good guesses. I would imagine it is something expensive, something you've hinted that you'd like to have, something that an old man would delight in giving his beautiful young—"

"Stop, that's quite enough."

"He's probably bought you an airplane now, too," Brett laughed cynically. "In red, perhaps, to match your new yacht."

Molly stood up, her head reeling after Brett's cutting remarks. She couldn't stand to listen to any more, and the prospect of six hours aboard the *Princess* with him tonight sickened her. It would be six hours of his taunts and his unfair vilification. She grabbed her windbreaker from the chair beside her and threaded her way out of the room through the adjoining tables. She hurried down the steps and out into the night, pausing for just a moment to slip into the jacket. She was struggling to connect the zipper through eyes too misted by tears to see clearly, when she heard Brett bound down the steps behind her.

"Running away from me again?" he said harshly.

"No I'm not running away. I promised to have dinner with you, and dinner is over and I've had it."

"You forced me to leave before the waitress brought my change. Now I've left an overly-generous tip."

"I'm sure you can afford it."

"It seems I am always running after you. Today you led me on a merry chase in that jeep."

"You didn't need to come after me then, and you don't need to come after me now."

"I think you enjoy being chased, don't you?"

"No I don't!"

"You are one of those girls who likes to play hard-to-get."

"I am not one of 'those girls' as you are always trying to label me, and I am not playing at anything. I *am* hard to get."

"Not for certain people. People who've paid you their dues."

"Look, as hard as this is for you to believe, I'm not owned by anyone. I have no special ties to Mr.

Gunther, other than my appreciation to him for offering me a job and for having the patience to teach it to me."

"And you have lots of clever ways of showing your appreciation, I'm sure. But those clever little ways of yours are for Mr. Leland Gunther, and only Mr. Gunther, aren't they?"

"Why do you care?" She tossed her head to free her hair from the base of her neck where it was pressing hotly. "Why do you persist in torturing me when I've tried over and over to convince you that you're wrong?"

She spoke so passionately that she was afraid she was attracting the attention of passersby. Brett seemed surprised by the tremble in her voice that gave hint that she might soon lose control of herself altogether.

He took her by the arm and led her away from the after-dinner crowds and over toward the benched seawall that was almost completely engulfed in darkness.

"Now calm down, will you?" he asked gently, showing for the first time that he might regret having pushed her so far with his condemning words.

"I never lost my temper in my whole life until I met you," she said. "But you have done nothing but criticize me and judge me since that first moment I met you on your boat. You drive me crazy."

"You tend to drive me a little crazy, too," he said. "I've said too much. It's none of my business how you lead your life." She saw him rubbing his hands across his face in exasperation with himself, and she was surprised to see some evidence that he could feel remorse.

"Come on," he said, starting to move in the direction of the pier. "We have our orders. Let's just put this subject behind us and get ready for our midnight sail. Maybe those are good winds up there. Maybe they'll blow away all your anger." He was looking up at the bank of clouds being tugged by the jetstream across the island and toward Los Angeles.

So that was it. He would offer her no apology, he wouldn't admit to any mistake in his opinions. He thought that a good brisk breeze filling the sails could cure her momentary pique, and make her forgive and forget whatever pain he might have unfeelingly inflicted.

"Brett, I don't care what you believe about me. I only know that I don't want to hear any more of it. And I can't stand to be around anyone who has such a low opinion of me. You can sail the boat back by yourself. I'm not going."

"What do you mean?" he asked.

"I can catch the seaplane or the helicopter in the morning and be home in fifteen minutes."

"Without having to spend another night on the boat with me?"

"Exactly."

He slumped slightly, and his voice indicated she had exhausted him with the fury she'd generated. "I don't know why you feel you can't trust me. I read your 'hands off' messages loud and clear. But if that's your decision, then I'll not run after you anymore."

"Thank you for that." She turned to walk away, hoping to lose herself in the people walking by and get away from him before he could hurt her anymore. Just as she stepped into a bright circle of light beneath a lamppost, she felt his grip on her shoulder and he spun her around to face him.

"I'll say good-bye to you right here then. A sailor about to venture into a storm deserves that at least."

Before she could avoid what was coming he had taken her brazenly into his arms and was kissing her with cruel, possessive lips. His unshaven cheeks felt harsh against her face, and as she tried to twist away from him they scratched at her as if to punish her for her resistance.

She could hear two teenagers on skateboards whiz past on each side of them. They whistled and jeered, making fun of the couple they'd barely missed. She knew that Brett was making a public spectacle of her, showing the world that he considered her common property, a woman who made herself available for any man to take his pleasure.

He knew that amid the chuckles of the strangers around them, she could not fight him as she wanted to. She pushed him away, her face contorted with the physical and mental pain his kiss had caused her. If he had intended to plummet her into the depths of shame, he had succeeded. She felt as cheapened as if his image of her were true.

He walked away from her, and she slunk into the shadows nearby and watched his long strides eat up the sidewalk quickly. As he stepped onto the pier she expected him to turn back and give her a last look of victory, but he strode right on out of her view as if he were anxious to forget her. He knew that he had paid her in kind for her desertion. A crew member who jumps ship does not go unpunished by Captain Sterling.

Chapter Five

When Molly got to her room, she was still breathing fast from the climb up the hill. She had hurried all the way, for the high winds had brought more clouds over the island, and by the time she undressed for bed and drew the curtains back to look at the harbor it had started to rain. She stared intently through the drizzly darkness and thought she saw the glow of lights where the *Princess* was docked.

It depressed her to think how Brett's shattering kiss had so demoralized her. She felt drained of all her will to fight him back, and she was glad she had already convinced him she would not sail back with him before he had startled her with his brutally aggressive act. She was not so sure she could stand up to him so firmly now. She would probably crumple before him, unwilling to be his, but no longer full of the energizing rage with which to strike out at him. She had underestimated his thirst to have his own way. He had tricks up his sleeve with which to defeat her every attempt to hold him off.

She rubbed one finger absently across her bruised lips, still tender from the effects of his kiss, and wondered what he was doing now. He was probably preparing for departure. He would have the generator going and all the lights on. He would be putting on his foul weather gear. Then he would drag out the sail bags from their bins, probably cursing her all the while for leaving him to do it alone.

She got into bed, leaving the drape open so that she wouldn't miss any changes in the weather, and fell into a heavy sleep almost at once. She awakened with a start, dreaming that someone was taking flashbulb photos of her, exploding the bright bursts of light right into her face. Then she realized that lightning was streaking across the sky outside her window. She jumped out of bed in time to hear the boom of the accompanying thunder.

It was still raining, now so heavily that she could see nothing of the boats in the harbor. This was no light sprinkle, it was a heavy downpour, and though she had just emerged from a warm bed her whole body felt instantly clammy with fear.

Brett could not manage that boat alone, even in the clearest of weather. Why hadn't she thought of that when she walked off and left him? She should have realized that he was obsinate enough to go ahead and attempt the trip without her. Sailing at night, through complete darkness, would require one person on constant watch, but he was alone and couldn't be two places at once. And could he trust the radar equipment? She remembered that he told her at dinner that it was now working, but what if he'd been wrong, or just trying to reassure her that together they could manage the trip home in the dark which Leland had ordered them to make?

She turned on the small portable heater in her room because her bare feet felt icy. Then she pulled a chair close to the window and wrapped herself in a blanket to sit and keep watch. But she knew that she belonged on the *Princess* where she could help Brett. By now he was probably halfway across the channel, and in this weather he would not be able to sight either shore.

How alone he must feel! If she were with him, she could bring him coffee, keep her eye on the radar, or stand at the bow and watch for landfall. But in her hotel room she was helpless, unable to do anything but watch and wait.

She knew that if anything happened to Brett, she would never forgive herself for her childish tantrum. She should have been mature enough to realize that she had responsibilities which she had to fulfill. When Leland and Mac had been unable to accompany them, she had assured Brett that she could crew for him. And now she had abandoned him when he most needed her help.

She sat huddled in misery throughout the rest of the night, constantly reiterating all the dangers that lay in wait for Brett. And she clung to small hopes. Brett was an experienced sailor. The *Princess* was exceptionally seaworthy. And perhaps, just perhaps, Brett had decided not to leave at all. Maybe he was more content than she was at this moment, sleeping below decks on the pitching *Princess* right down there in the harbor.

Just before dawn the rain slowed its pace and she fell asleep for awhile in her chair. Then she awakened to stare out at the heavy mist the rain had left behind, and drift again into a troubled sleep. The next time she awakened to take a weather check the sky was beginning to lighten, but she still could not make out any boats in the harbor because her visibility was now hampered by the same morning fog that had troubled her yesterday when she had rowed away from Brett and her unreliable instincts.

She should have had more confidence in her own self-control. Surely she could have resisted Brett's amorous advances, she could have made him understand that she was not going to let him carry out his romantic weekend plans for her. And then she would have been with him to help him weather this night.

She shook off the blanket and fumbled through the half-light to find some warm clothes. As soon as the soggy morning was firmly established she packed up her things and prepared to leave her vigil and take some action. She would go to the Harbormaster's office and make him radio the marina, and she would wait there with him until there was word that Brett had made it safely across. Just making the plans encouraged her. Soon all the worry would be over. If the fog cleared as it had yesterday morning, she would be on a plane and home in time to wash down the decks for Brett and assure him that she had not completely forgotten her duties. No matter what he thought of her as a person, she was determined to win his forgiveness for her lapse of sailing manners. It was more important to her than ever that he acknowledge her as a good crew member.

Molly walked out to the very end of the fog-locked pier, assuring herself that the Harbormaster would be there to help her. She was certain that the Harbor Patrol must be on duty all night. They had to be available for rescues and other emergencies. She prayed that she wouldn't discover that the beautiful *Princess* had had to sound a cry for their assistance during the storm.

The big windows of the bright green building were ablaze with lights and inside she could see a uniformed man at his desk.

"I'm looking for Brett Sterling," she blurted out as soon as she entered the office. "He's aboard the *Princess,* and I want to know if he left last night for the mainland."

"I sure hope not," the man answered with professional cool. "That storm kicked up quite a fuss. There were some pretty big swells here in the harbor. I was afraid we were going to have to tow some of these boats into calmer waters."

"Then you don't know—you can't tell me where he is?"

"Well, he came in here last night pretty late and we talked about the weather. I advised him to wait until daybreak to set off. He was looking for someone to crew with him. He wanted to find that boy who often sails with him. What's his name, Chuck?"

"I don't know. I was supposed to crew for him, and I—well, I—lost touch with him."

"I wouldn't be the least bit worried about Brett if he were in his own boat. When he's at the helm of the *Pleasure Seeker,* there's no weather that can hold him back, but that new boat he's trying out is too big to handle alone. Even if he found Chuck, I hope they decided to wait for the clearing."

The man behind the desk had swung into action even while he was calmly chatting with Molly. He was twisting the dials on the radio communication equipment beside him.

"I'll just get my patrol boat to run over and look for Mr. Sterling," he said to Molly as he awaited an answer to his summons. "Pete, take a look at number 139 and see if Brett Sterling has left the harbor yet, will you? It's still too foggy to eyeball him from here."

There was a crackle and a pop from the radio as the patrolman responded, then Molly heard a motor rev into action as it moved away.

After a few minutes of anxious finger-tapping, Molly heard a voice on the radio. "The *Princess* is still in number 139. But I think Brett Sterling went ashore about an hour ago. Do you want me to find him? He's probably having breakfast somewhere."

"Negative. Just come and pick up his crew."

He turned to give Molly a big smile. "That's what you want, isn't it? A lift out to the boat where you're supposed to be?"

Molly was so relieved she could hardly think of an answer for him. She hadn't thought about what she would do if she found Brett still here in the bay. But she had promised herself that she would never again neglect her duties as first mate, so she nodded almost automatically.

"Pete will pick you up right down there," the Harbormaster said, indicating a ramp off the pier. "If this fog breaks up like it did yesterday, you'll have a fine day for your return trip."

"Thank you," Molly stammered, knowing there were no words sufficient to express her gratitude. She felt as if he had loosened a tremendous load she'd been carrying on her shoulders all night long. And there was a lightness to her step as she bounded toward the waiting patrol boat.

"Isn't it a beautiful day?" she asked the patrolman as he helped her aboard. "Everything smells so fresh after the rain. I love mornings like this."

The astounded man looked around him at the fog-locked harbor and said nothing.

Molly felt that even though Brett would not be there, a brass band should be waiting to pipe her aboard the *Princess*. There should be music and cheers to welcome her home, at the very least, she laughed to herself. But the decks were empty and quiet, as if the *Princess* were dozing in the still water after a night of tempestuous disco dancing with the swells.

She stowed her gear in the locker in her own cabin and then wandered through the cozy spaces that had once seemed so confining to her. She opened the door into the master cabin and noted that the bed had been slept in; the sheets still bore the rumpled imprint of Brett's body.

She saw his shaving gear, still moist from use, spread out on a teak-lipped counter over his sink. And she couldn't resist reaching over to take his bottle of shaving cologne. She brought it close to her face, inhaling the familiar scent around the loosened cap. Holding the bottle she sat down on the still-warm bed and wondered when he would return. She glanced at a rolled up sweater beside the bed, a sailing magazine that was propped in the reading rack, all his things waiting in lonely silence for his return. Only his compelling presence would bring all these things to life once again.

She tightened the cap on the cologne bottle and put it back where she'd found it, reluctant to let go of the evocative memories it had brought back to her. She was flooded with her feelings of relief that Brett was all right. The thought that he was at this moment enjoying ham and eggs somewhere brought a smile to her lips. And she wondered how she could feel such tenderness for a man who had no respect for her at all. There was nothing about her way of life that he admired, his attitude toward her had been consistently grating, and yet knowing that he was safe from danger had made her morning joyous.

She went out on deck to await his return, confident that he would accept her apology for the moments of anger last night. She was determined the cruise home would be uneventful and free of dissen-sion. She wanted nothing to destroy her happy mood.

The boats around her were beginning to show signs of life as people came out on their decks to take a reading of the weather and plan their day. The shoreboat had begun the regular run and was bring-ing life to the tranquil harbor with comings and goings. She heard a noisy outboard motor propelling a bright orange rubber dinghy toward her from the pier, and then she realized that Brett might have added the motor to the boat she had rowed yester-day.

As it drew closer, Molly could see that it con-tained two men, so that if this was Brett, he was bringing someone with him. Maybe he had found the crewman he had been looking for, his friend Chuck. Molly stepped down into the companionway so that she could watch the approach unobserved, and within a few seconds she had no doubts that the wide-shouldered figure guiding the boat was Brett Sterling. He was wearing a classic Navy pea coat of dark blue, buttoned double-breasted across his broad chest against the cold morning. And on his head he sported a Greek fisherman's cap of dark wool that made him seem even more the imposing seaman. The boy beside him was more slightly built, with straight blond hair that was, like Brett's, in need of a trim and blowing about his ears in the wind.

Suddenly Molly had doubts. She could not antici-pate what Brett's reaction would be to her unex-pected reappearance. And she did not want to pro-voke him to further insults in front of this stranger. How could she explain to him why she'd had a change of heart and decided to come along after all?

She hurried down the steps out of their sight, and

as she heard them pull alongside she went into her cabin and closed the door. After awhile she heard the two of them come below to attend to some business at the chart table, and she cautiously opened the door and stepped out into the main salon.

Brett was bent over the radio trying to bring in some weather news, and the boy looked up and saw Molly and gave her a startled look.

"Hey, Brett, there's a stowaway on board," he exclaimed.

Brett spun around and saw her. "What are you doing here?" he asked her, his attitude less than cordial.

"I had promised to crew for you and I intend to live up to that promise."

"That's not what you said last night."

"I may be a little late, but I'm reporting for duty."

"Well, you are too late. I spent half the night finding a replacement for you. This is Chuck Yancey. Chuck, this is the one I was telling you about: Molly Weston."

"How do you do, Miss Weston. Glad to have you aboard. We can use the extra hands." Chuck's wide smile and friendly acceptance were in stark contrast to Brett's tight-lipped bad humor.

"For your information," Brett directed his comments to Molly over his shoulder as he gave his primary attention to the radio set at the navigator's table, "Chuck had planned this vacation a long time ago. He was camping out with friends over at Two Harbors and it took some pretty fancy detective work to find him and get him here."

"I can imagine," she said, trying to give her words just the right touch of awe that would perhaps flatter Brett into a more conciliatory mood. But her attempt did not reach the target.

"Now we've cut off his vacation plans for nothing. If I'd known you were going to indulge in a capricious change of mind this morning, I wouldn't have had to fetch Chuck. You are all the crew I would have needed."

"Aw, Brett. It's kind of fun to have a pretty helper like Molly on board. And my vacation was already ruined by the rainstorm. Have you ever slept all night in a soggy sleeping bag?" Chuck asked Molly with a merry smile.

"As a matter of fact, I have," she said, reminded again of her night spent with Brett up on deck beneath his damp sleeping bag. "I know how unpleasant that can be," she added, hoping Brett would know what she was thinking of. But Brett seemed impervious to any hurt she might try to inflict.

"Chuck, you go check the bilge," Brett ordered, terse as usual. "And Molly, ready the storm sails in case we run into more squalls. I'll have to radio our ETA to the marina. And I'll have them get in touch with Mr. Gunther and let him know we won't be arriving this morning as he ordered."

"You haven't called him yet?" Molly asked, concerned that her busy employer would make an unnecessary early-morning trip to the dock only to be disappointed.

"I've been a little too busy to worry about your Mr. Gunther. He is not as constantly on my mind as he is on yours." Brett turned to look at her, his sea-blue eyes now cold and stormy.

"When do you think we'll reach the marina?" she asked.

"About three or four this afternoon with the gusty winds I'm expecting. If Mr. Gunther can take the time to inspect the *Princess* this afternoon, she'll be available for him. If he can't, then that is his problem."

"Aren't you forgetting that you are the one trying to sell the boat? I should think you would try to arrange things for his convenience."

"Thinking of Mr. Gunther's convenience is your job, Miss Weston, and I'm sure you do it quite well. And speaking of your job, hadn't you better get up to those sail bins?"

Brett hunched his big shoulders over the radio set, and began expertly tuning in the channel that would enable him to send a message to the mainland. Acknowledging her dismissal, Molly left him to tend to her duties.

As she struggled with the heavy sail bags she repeated over and over to herself her vow to maintain a peaceful truce with Brett Sterling. It wouldn't be easy, but she must learn to ignore his jibes, and not respond. He had said that she was all the crew he would have needed on the trip home, and that was the compliment she had sought from him. She would have to remember that understated praise, and cherish it. No matter what he thought of her as a person, at least he had admitted that she was an adequate sailing companion.

Brett remained below decks at the radio for quite some time while Chuck and Molly readied the boat for departure, working with unspoken respect for each other's obvious competence at boat handling. Molly's face glowed with the fine layer of perspiration that denoted hard physical labor. But she was rewarded with Brett's look of admiration when he finally came topside.

"Everything's done? Well, I guess two deckhands are better than one. Now we have time for a cup of coffee while we wait for the last of this fog to burn off."

"I'll get it, Captain," Chuck said as his lean body sprang for the companionway hatch.

"I got a message back from Mr. Gunther, Molly," Brett said when they were alone in the cockpit. "Just as I suspected, he won't be able to spend any time on the *Princess* this afternoon."

"Oh, really? That's too bad."

"It seems that this surprise he's cooked up for you requires all his attention. He took great pains to remind me that he had this morning scheduled for boat shopping, and he was quite miffed that the weather had not cooperated with his plans."

Molly had never known Mr. Gunther to be miffed with anything, and she knew him to be too much of a gentleman to have complained on the public channels of the radiophone because of anything as unpredictable as a weather delay. But if that was the interpretation Brett cared to give Mr. Gunther's remarks, she would not question it.

"Do you want me to make up the sandwiches now, so we can eat in shifts, whenever we have time?"

"You're really anxious to get back, aren't you? I suppose you can't wait to find out what this surprise is that he's bought for you."

"I'm hoping that the surprise is the news that he's sold off one of his companies. That was the business deal that kept him from coming along with us this weekend."

"If he sells a company, he'll have a great deal more ready cash, won't he?" Brett said.

"Mr. Gunther doesn't need money. He needs more time for leisure and relaxation. He's reached the age when he needs to slow down a bit and enjoy life."

"And he's found someone to enjoy that luxurious life with him, hasn't he?"

"I'll go below and get busy in the galley now, if you'll excuse me." She ducked her head to hide her hurt expression from his scrutiny.

"You're not going to give me your usual angry denials?" Brett seemed disappointed that he had not ignited the sparks of controversy between them that usually resulted in an unpleasant fiery scene. For some perverse reason he seemed to enjoy baiting her, and she now realized that she could frustrate him the most by refusing to answer his unfair charges. If only she had learned that technique earlier, she could have saved herself a lot of expended emotion.

They were ready to depart when the fog cleared. Brett stayed at the wheel and motored them out of the harbor, and then at his instruction, Molly and Chuck winched the sails up and Brett turned off the engine. With the noxious odor of the diesel fumes extinguished, and the throbbing sound of the engines no longer assaulting their ears, they could begin to enjoy the sensations of being under sail.

Brett sat on the transom, his heavy coat open now that the weather was warming, his light eyes narrowed as he studied the telltale that wriggled from the shroud and gave him instant clues as to the nature of the winds that powered his vessel.

Molly wriggled out of her heavy sweater so that she could enjoy the crisp day in the cotton T-shirt that she had worn beneath it. Then she put on some dark glasses and went to the foredeck and sat leaning against the mast, her legs stretched out in front of her. She watched the seagulls who pursued them from Avalon like camp followers, swooping down at their wake. As they pulled farther away from the island, the flock of birds thinned out until only one or two hardy hopefuls remained to scold them for their lack of garbage donations. At last even they returned to scavenger the more promising sands back at the beach.

Now that Chuck had checked every winch, he

sprawled out on the foredeck beside Molly, curving himself comfortably around an open hatch that protruded into his way. Brett would have slammed the hatch closed, she mused, demanding that it accommodate him. But Chuck did not seem to have the same need to fight the craft. He lounged with his head supported on one bent arm, looking up at Molly with interest.

"Where did you learn to sail? You really seem to know what you're doing!"

"I'm from Massachusetts. We are put into sail-boats back there before we're put onto tricycles. My boss is interested in buying this boat. So, I'm here to try it out."

"Well, if Brett recommends this boat, you can be sure it's a good one. He really knows his boats. I should know. I work for him, I'm on his payroll full-time. I ferry the boats around, and do some of the maintenance work. I just happened to be on vacation this week."

"Look, I am truly sorry about the mix-up."

"That's OK. I was planning to come home anyway today or tomorrow. I don't like to leave my sister alone for too long."

"Your sister?"

"Yeah, Rita. She works for Brett, too."

"I think I met her at Brett's penthouse." Remembering the blonde girl's lazy attitude Molly asked, "What exactly does she do?"

"Oh, she's sort of a secretary, and she crews sometimes. But she's not really as interested in boats as I am."

Molly was sure the girl didn't have to do much to earn her keep. She apparently had ways of keeping Brett satisfied that didn't require much knowledge of typing, shorthand or sail winching.

"So she's your sister," Molly was thinking out

loud. Now that she knew, she could see a startling resemblance between the two. But while Chuck had an honest open face that clearly showed his contentment with life and his cheerful nature, the girl had had a disturbing aura of wildness about her, a quality of excitability held barely in check. Her intense eyes had seemed to cry out for someone to bring her under control, and of course Brett would be the perfect person to understand that volatile kind of person. He was himself somewhat like a dormant volcano, smoldering away beneath the sight of the innocent people who could be destroyed by his next eruption. They were a perfectly matched pair.

"Brett's been awfully good to both of us," Chuck said, almost in answer to Molly's thoughts. "When he found us, we were broke and I was pretty disgusted with the kind of life we were living. You see, we were runaways. Some people think that's freedom, but there's no freedom when you're always wondering where you can find someone to give you your next meal."

"And Brett found you?" Molly asked. She could imagine how agreeable Brett had been to giving shelter to a beautiful and vulnerable girl like Rita. Especially when she had a hardworking brother who would be an asset to anyone's crew.

"When Brett hired me at his boatyard, I was happy to take on a steady job."

"Well, he certainly has the resources to help you," she said, meaning that with his money it was no sacrifice to take on two young people. But Chuck interpreted her words differently.

"You're right! He is the kindest man I've ever met. He always has time to listen to our problems. And I can tell you Rita and I have given him some worries. But he's been more than fair with us."

"How understanding Brett is," she said with great sarcasm, which Chuck missed.

"I think he understands our problems because he ran away himself when he was young. Only he joined the Navy and then he found Mac as a kind of substitute father. He didn't get along with his own father."

Molly was intrigued with the story, but she didn't want to pry. Fortunately, Chuck did not wait for any cue to continue the story.

"His father was a widower and he had a lot of money. But he just used the money to play around, you know?"

"A girl in every port?"

"That's what I mean," Chuck said with relief, not wanting to put into exact words the philandering nature of Brett's father. "Then when Brett's father died, he left his inheritance to Brett, and look what Brett's done with it."

"He's built up quite a little empire there at the marina, hasn't he?" she said.

"He's made a real success of his life, and I intend to do that, too, with his help."

"He seems to find the time for recreation."

"But don't you see? What he really wanted was to stay at sea, but he accepted the responsibility. He took his father's money and did something constructive with it. And now he can use it to help other people. He says in another year or two he's going to set me up in my own business, a boatyard of my own. Now isn't that something!"

Somewhat begrudgingly, Molly had to admit to Brett's generosity. Perhaps there was more to him than she had seen.

"Brett is most happy when he's like this," Chuck said, sitting up to point to the stern where Brett was studying the compass and adjusting the wheel to keep them on course.

Brett glanced up to see his two crew members turned around to look at him, and he gave them a sunny smile that seemed to confirm what Chuck had just said. There was no doubt in Molly's mind that he did seem more at home on a ship than he would be behind a desk or in a business meeting. And yet, he had forced himself to make a success of his investment career.

Chuck went on, apparently tireless when it came to extolling the virtues of his hero.

"Brett never complains, but I can tell that he's sometimes discontented. Whenever he has a really tough decision to make, or a problem that he can't solve, he takes off in the *Pleasure Seeker* and we don't see him for awhile. I think at times like that he'd like to disappear over the horizon and look for some happiness of his own. He deserves it."

Molly didn't say a word in response. She wanted to absorb this new information about Brett, and think about this man who had only shown her the fun-loving side of his personality.

"I think Brett wants something," Chuck said, waving back to him.

"Let me go," she said. "I think it's time for lunch."

"Then I'll take a short snooze," Chuck said, stretching out on his back with a yawn.

The ocean swells pushed the *Princess* up and down under her feet as Molly made her way back to the cockpit.

"Why don't you get us a couple of beers from the fridge?" Brett called to her when she was close enough to hear.

More to be companionable than because she felt

any craving for the drink on an empty stomach, she fetched two brown bottles of Mexican beer from the galley, opened them, and brought one to Brett.

"So you're going to join me?" he said with a smile.

"Yes, I even brought along a sandwich. Would you like to share it?"

"No, after you're finished I'll let you have the wheel and I'll take a break. One of those sandwiches of your requires total concentration."

Brett tipped his head back and took a long drink from the frost-coated bottle. She watched him with fascination, forgetting to eat or drink herself as she studied his ability to extract pleasure from the simplest small acts. Now that she understood him better, she knew that perhaps he had to. Perhaps his opportunities for real happiness were too few. He nudged her leg with his knee, and she realized she had been staring.

"Drink up, matey," he said with a laugh into the wind.

She looked down at his leg, bare beneath the cuff of his shorts, and close beside hers as they sat together on the transom. She could feel the tickle of those fine blond hairs that dusted his skin, attracting the sun so that his legs seemed to glisten with brilliance. His thighs were massive, muscular from the physical activity that he so enjoyed. And from the flexing strength of those thighs energy seemed to be transmitted upward throughout his body, right up to his hands where they gripped the wide varnished wheel. She could almost envision his personal electricity pouring through his hands, via the wheel, to the rudder that set the boat in the direction he wanted. From the leg that bumped suggestively against hers as the boat rocked back into a heeling position, to the full fifty-eight feet of boat they occupied, he was extending his mastery and loving it.

Realizing that Chuck had forced her to revise her opinions about Brett, she wondered if she could force upon Brett the same open-mindedness. If she were to try calmly, and without emotion, to explain her situation to him, would he give her a chance? Would he be willing to throw off his misconceptions, and take a look at the truth?

She finished off her sandwich as she rehearsed her speeches. The tangy beer tasted good to her after she'd eaten, and she sipped it in rather genteel imitation of Brett's way of drinking with complete abandon, his head thrown back to capture every drop. Just as she was ready to begin, he stood up, and taking hold of both of her shoulders, he slid her over the cushion so that she was sitting in the indentations that had been carved by his body into the padded vinyl.

"You take the wheel, helmsman. I'm going below and have a bite of lunch. Just keep her on that course. If the wind changes, I'll feel it and come change the sail setting."

He didn't return for about fifteen minutes, and by the time he was back behind the wheel the sun was brilliant. He had removed his heavy jacket, but he still wore the dark cap with the visor that protected his face from the sun. He turned his face from side to side as if he could check the subtleties of the wind with his very skin surfaces.

"I think Chuck is going to stay conked out until we hit the breakwater," he said.

"You're very fond of him, aren't you?"

"He's a wonderful kid."

"And his sister?" she ventured.

"I've had some problems with both of them. They

weren't used to applying their own self-discipline when I first met them. But they're learning."

"From what Chuck has told me, you've been like a father to them."

"Well, I guess I have in a way," he acknowledged.

"Then will you try to give me some of that same understanding?"

"What do you mean?"

"I'm going to make one last attempt to defend myself to you. And you can believe me, or not, as you wish."

"Is it so important to you?" He took his eyes off the water ahead to turn and look into hers. Again, she noticed the creamy tan of his skin, with the fine network of weather-lines etched around his eyes.

"I told you that I don't care what you think," she said, "but I guess I do."

"Then state your case."

"It's about Mr. Gunther. You see, he and my father were business associates. He bought my father's company many years ago, and kept him on to run it for him. He often came to visit us, he became a family friend. But my father took some business risks on his own and didn't tell Leland—that is, Mr. Gunther—about them."

"Go ahead, you can call him Leland if you want."

"Well, anyway, before long it became clear that my father was in big financial trouble. He lost almost everything, and of course Leland now owned his company, so by the time he died we had nothing left."

"But Leland wasn't responsible?"

"No, he wasn't. But he blamed himself. He felt that if he'd allowed my father to confide in him more, he might have learned of his troubles in time to save him. Leland is the kind of a man who wants to help, and in this case he wasn't able to. He stayed in touch with Mom and me, checking up on us to make sure we had enough to live on. And he saw to it that I got a scholarship so I could go to college."

"I see. The concerned family friend."

Molly couldn't see Brett's expression, for his cap shaded his face, but his voice gave her the first hint of sympathy she'd ever had from him.

"He came east to attend my graduation, and he offered me a job working for him. And my mother agreed to let me come out here, but only after Leland promised to look after me as he would his own daughter."

"So you're saying he became a substitute father to you, is that it?"

"He could never replace my own father. He had been a strong man, and I looked up to him. But I was used to having someone look after me, and Leland took on that responsibility."

"Take off your dark glasses. I can't see your eyes," Brett said abruptly. She did as he asked.

"You are telling me that your relationship with Leland Gunther is based entirely on friendship, that the only reason he appears to want to do so much for you is because he wants to make it up to you for what happened to your father?"

"Yes, that's what I'm telling you. Now, can you believe it?" Molly asked, her voice trembling.

"I know it is possible," he answered quietly.

"Can't you believe that a man would do such generous things for me and ask nothing in return?"

"I can believe that someone would want to do generous things for you. But if it were me, I'd ask for a lot in return." His voice was husky, but the words were spoken in such a low tone that Molly could barely hear him over the bombarding sea sounds around them.

"Maybe you would—," Molly began, wondering

with a fearful heart if he still would persist in his disbelief. But he interrupted her by taking his hands from the wheel and wrapping his arms around her in an embrace. As she relaxed in his arms, he took hold of her chin and tipped her head back to look into her eyes.

After a searching look he gently placed his lips on the side of her face, then moved them slowly to a spot on her neck where her blood throbbed fast and hot just beneath the skin. At last he found her lips, and he kissed her languorously, with no urgency, no demands upon her. It was a communicative kiss, and it spoke of understanding and compassion, and she dared to hope it was a kiss that asked for forgiveness. She was certain he was telling her he knew now that he had been wrong about her. For the first time she could respond to him freely. She placed her hands around his neck, her lips parted as she luxuriated in the new sensations Brett was offering her.

The jealous *Princess*, now left untended, tried to attract their attention. She threw herself sharply over a swell, hoping to draw Brett's guiding hands back to her. But instead he let the lurch of the boat push him back onto the transom cushions, and Molly fell softly and willingly on top of him. The more the craft pitched and rolled to distract them, the more closely it pressed their bodies together. The provocative rise and fall of the surface beneath them added new dimensions of feeling that both were unwilling to forsake. Finally, the *Princess* gave up, and steadied herself to wait patiently for them.

Molly pulled her lips from Brett's a mere inch, and looked down into the blueness of his eyes which seemed deep enough to swim in. Then her eyes were drawn to his lips as they slowly curved upward into a satisfied smile, and she felt a craving to feel their enrapturing touch again.

But out of the corner of her eye she noticed some movement, and before she could return to the promise of the moment, she turned to see that Chuck had moved to a sitting position on the foredeck, and with his back turned to them was rubbing at his face. She pulled away from Brett and sat up, patting at her hair.

Brett refused to be disturbed from his position. He remained, spread-eagled on his back, his arms suspended in midair as if she were still in his grasp.

"Get up," Molly gasped at him, putting her dark glasses back on. But Chuck ambled loosely toward the stern with a sleepy look devoid of comprehension.

"What time is it? I'm kind of hungry," he mumbled.

"It's time for you to eat. And make it snappy," Brett said, sitting up. "We'll be hitting the breakwater pretty soon and I'll need your help."

Scratching at his disheveled hair, Chuck disappeared below. Molly moved closer to Brett as soon as Chuck was gone, but knowing that the boy might reappear at any moment seemed to have put an effective damper on Brett's lovemaking.

"Molly, I've never wanted to hurt you. And I don't want to hurt you now, but I have to give you some advice, and I don't think you'll like it."

Molly stiffened.

"If what you've told me is the truth, I think you should give up your job with Mr. Gunther. You've told me how important your reputation is to you, and if I suspected the worst of Mr. Gunther's intentions, others may do the same."

"But he needs me right now. He's very lonely, and he's trying to decide what to do with the rest of his life."

"That's just it. You may consider your relationship with him completely innocent, but others may not see it that way. And it is just possible that Mr. Gunther doesn't see it that way."

"You're wrong about that. I know that you're wrong."

"Then you won't consider it?"

"No, I won't. I love my job. and I owe it to Leland to stick with him when he needs me."

Brett sat silently brooding, obviously not used to people balking at his suggestions. Then she realized that he was asking her for proof. If she were not physically involved with Mr. Gunther, she was to quit her job and leave him, just to prove she was not lying.

Chuck came out to pull down the sails and Molly made no move to help him. She huddled close to Brett on his leeward side, wishing there was more time to talk to him. She wished she knew how to interpret his kiss. Did he mean it to convey that he believed her, or just that he wanted to believe her but that he still had doubts?

But Brett was now busy navigating the boat through the boat traffic of Marina del Rey. And as they neared the Sterling Anchorage she slipped away from him to go below and collect her gear.

She came topside again just as Brett was expertly inching the boat up to his dock. Molly was startled to see two familiar figures standing on the dock waiting for them, chatting together as if they'd been friends their whole lives. It was Mac, waiting to greet Brett, and Leland Gunther waiting for Molly. For once in her life Molly was not happy to see her employer. The fact that he was waiting here for Molly would just reinforce Brett's suspicions, and she winced as Leland called out excitedly,

"There's my girl, back from her voyage with roses in her cheeks."

As soon as Brett had turned off the engine he jumped onto the dock and greeted Mac with a bear hug. Then he turned coldly to Mr. Gunther.

"Can you spare just a moment to come on board and look over the *Princess.*"

"Young man, I have only one thing on my mind right now. And that's to spirit your pretty passenger away from you as fast as possible."

"Oh, really?" Brett's eyes narrowed menacingly, and Molly hurried to step onto the dock and try to keep the peace. "I want you to know that I've gone to a great deal of trouble entertaining Miss Weston, making this yacht available for your inspection."

Leland seemed blind to the discord he was creating. "Well, I've gone to a lot of trouble to arrange a special treat for Miss Weston, myself. And if we don't get going right this minute, I just may burst wide open with the waiting." Then he took Molly completely by surprise by lifting her off her feet in his arms. "Welcome home, sweetheart," he shouted, puckering up to give her a noisy kiss.

"Brett, we can't tarry here long with putting the *Princess* right," Mac said to his friend, obviously wondering why Brett was so stiffly attentive. "I put together a pot of chicken chowder for supper, and Rita gave me orders to get you and Chuck home for it by six."

Molly pulled herself from the grasp of Leland's bony fingers to turn toward Brett. He made no secret of the fact that he had been watching her embrace with Leland. He was standing with his arms folded arrogantly across his chest.

He had told her he didn't want to come home to the things he hated. Now she knew what he'd been talking about. It was Leland Gunther, and Molly's supposedly immoral relationship with him, that Brett couldn't face.

Chapter Six

"Give your things to Mr. Perkins, dear. I want you to come in my car with me," Leland said.

Molly was too preoccupied to be curious. "But—"

"We'll pick up the other car later. We aren't going far."

Leland was overly animated with excitement. The lethargy and depression that had worried Molly a few days ago seeming to have disappeared during her absence.

"I've planned a wonderful surprise for you. I think you'll be just tickled pink."

"Leland, you do too much for me. That camera was enough. Some people might get the wrong idea if you continue to shower me with surprises."

"Let people think what they will. It's been a long time since I've had someone to buy gifts for." He reached over to squeeze her hand, and Molly had a wave of apprehension as she remembered how care-

ful she had planned to be in handling his affection for
her.

She was tired from loss of sleep, but her hazy mind
formed a plan with which she might deflect him. She
thought she should remind him that she had a life of
her own with younger friends. She was not very
practiced in duplicity, but perhaps if she hinted that
Brett was interested in her he would get the idea that
he was too old to count on her as a companion
forever.

"I'm sorry you couldn't come along on the trip,
Leland. It was wonderful. Brett was quite nice
taking me along when you couldn't go."

"That chap seems a bit hard to get along with to
me."

"Oh, no. You're wrong about him. He's really
very nice. I like him."

She started to say more but she found that the
words choked her. How she would like to be able to
say that Brett liked her, too! That he respected her
and wanted to be with her. That they were in love.
That they were going to be married and spend the
rest of their lives together. But Brett did not feel that
way about her, and to pretend that he did was a
game too hurtful to continue.

"Now, don't tell me you've tamed that wild man
of the marina during those few hours at sea."

"I know he's quite a playboy, isn't he?"

"Yes, there aren't many pretty girls he's missed,
from what I've heard. But I imagine a sweet innocent little thing like yourself could quite sweep him
off his feet, if she tried."

If Leland knew what Brett thought of the sweet
little thing he so doted upon, he'd be so enraged he
would probably invite him out for a thrashing. But
she doubted that Leland's denials would be any
more effective with Brett than hers had been.

Whatever Leland Gunther's intentions toward her might be, she knew they were honorable, and only motivated by his need for someone to talk to. But there seemed no way to convince Brett Sterling of that.

"Take us right up to the main entrance of the Sterling Towers, Perkins," Leland instructed, and Molly wondered what that destination could have to do with the secret Leland was keeping.

Leland led the way out of the car and into the apartment complex. On the way up in the elevator he removed a new key ring from his pocket and began jingling the keys on it with a happy smile on his face that smoothed out every wrinkle. He watched Molly as if he wanted to be ready to soak up her appreciation the moment she saw the surprise.

Using the new keys, Leland opened the door into apartment 1103 and threw the door open to usher Molly inside.

"Well, what do you think? Isn't it a beauty? Decorated to the nines, and the last one available for lease in this building. Step over here and look at this view of the marina."

"It's gorgeous, Leland. But what is it for? Are you going to move here?"

He stepped over to her and stood with his lanky frame towering over her small one. He pulled her hand forward and dropped the keys into it.

"This apartment is for you. And it even comes with a roommate to keep you company."

Molly stared up into his face with a stricken look that widened her brown eyes. The keys felt like a cold heavy weight in her hand. Could she have misjudged this man who had seemed to her only a kindly benefactor and employer? Was it possible that Brett Sterling had been right, that Leland wanted to shower her with boats and luxurious apartments, anything she wanted, just to win her favors?

"What do you mean, a roommate?"

He was watching her with an eagerly expectant expression, but she looked away from him, her mind reeling. She had to get the matter out in the open, make him state his intentions right now so that she could set him straight. But she dreaded the prospect of hurting him, of losing his friendship forever.

"Now, Miss Molly, you were just telling me how some people get the wrong impression of things. How do you think it would look if I rented an expensive apartment down here where all the single swingers live, and if I came to call all the time?"

"Leland, don't say any more, please." As she struggled to think how she could tell him no, it occurred to her that the next worse thing would be telling Brett Sterling he had been right all along about Leland.

"But I've taken care of all that," he was saying. "Now when I come to call it will be to take two lovely ladies out to dinner."

Just then Molly heard the door behind her open, and a familiar mirth-filled voice exclaim, "Leland, you've teased her enough."

"Mother! What are you doing here?"

Molly ran over and threw herself into her mother's arms. Charlotte Weston looked younger and happier than when Molly had last seen her almost a year ago. Her once bright red hair was now streaked through with white, so that it seemed softer and lighter, and her skin glowed with the good health imparted to it by the long walks along the Massachusetts shore that she so loved.

"Your employer is a very persuasive man. He kept telling me that I should see California sometime, and that I ought to visit my daughter, and finally he just mailed me a ticket and said to come for the summer."

Molly looked from one to the other of them as they beamed across at each other, obviously proud of themselves for planning such a stunning surprise for her.

Leland raked his long white hair with his fingers, as if he were just a little embarrassed now to continue with his joke. "You see, I'll be coming here to take your mother sight-seeing, or to take her to some fancy restaurant, and I just thought you should be here with her. Kind of like a chaperone, you see?"

"I see. Oh, yes indeed. I see!" Molly collapsed onto the expensive white sofa, laughing with an almost hysterical relief. "And here I thought, I thought—"

"Now I'm going to leave you two girls alone together to get all of the jabbering out of your systems." He started for the door. "I hope you won't mind being moved out of the guest house down here to the marina for awhile, Molly dear. It's a longer drive to the office, but you won't be coming there very often while your mother's here. You're going to take some of that vacation you've earned."

Molly stood up and followed him, reaching out to stop him with a hand on his arm, her heart again wide open for him, with no more need to disguise her deep affection. How good it felt to know she hadn't lost the honest relationship she so cherished!

"Thank you for bringing mama out here. And thank you for being the wonderful man you are."

She wanted to tell him more. She wanted to apologize for thinking, just for a moment, that he could have ulterior motives for his generosity. But that was Brett Sterling's fault. He had made her as suspicious of people as he was. She could only have had that ugly premonition about Leland because she was looking at him with Brett's perverted viewpoint.

Leland led Molly outside the apartment door.

"I know there was a time when you and your mother didn't think I was so wonderful. I know you probably blamed me for your father's financial troubles. But I swear to you, Molly. I didn't know. If I'd only known, I would have tried to help. You explain that to her." He nodded his head toward the inside of the apartment where Molly's mother was.

"She knows, Leland, or she wouldn't have come out here at your invitation."

"That's why I'm just so all fired pleased that she came. Now that she's here maybe I can convince her I never meant any harm to come to your family."

"You come back here at eight o'clock tonight and start your convincing. After I go to the market mama is going to make us up a Yankee stew."

Leland stuffed his hands into his pants pockets and strode off toward the elevators with a galloping gait.

The next morning Charlotte and Molly Weston sat in their rumpled bathrobes having coffee together over the morning paper just as they had so often at home. But the setting was quite different. Instead of their darkly paneled little house, they were in a bright California apartment. And the weather outside was clear and hot, with none of the damp New England overcast they were so used to.

"I suspected that Leland was giving me a sales pitch when he told me you were homesick," Charlotte said with a fond chuckle. "I knew he wanted me out here for other reasons."

"What other reasons?"

"I could tell from the many long phone conversations that I've been having with Leland that he needed to feel forgiven. I know he feels guilty that he couldn't help."

Charlotte Weston was eyeing her daughter carefully. "Leland thought up this job for you as a way to get you out into the world. But has it made you happy, Molly? You look so preoccupied. Last night when Leland was here you kept staring out the window as though you weren't with us."

"I just need a change of pace. And having you here is a wonderful change. Now my life is complete." She refilled her mother's coffee cup.

"Is it? What about this Brett Sterling character that Leland spoke about last night?" Mrs. Weston looked curiously at her daughter.

"He's a business contact of Mr. Gunther's that I've had some dealings with," Molly said evasively. "He was just nice to me because he was trying to sell a boat and I'm afraid Mr. Gunther jumped to the wrong impression."

"I see. Well, Leland said to take all this week off and I hope you'll do that. He's going to show me around town so he won't need you at the office, I'm sure." Charlotte Weston jumped to her feet with a youthful fluster to her movements that Molly had rarely seen. "Oh, I'd better get dressed. It's almost noon. Are you coming with us?"

"No, I'm going to snoop around the marina a little bit, and have lunch by myself in the sun, while you two talk about the Fabulous Forties and other things I'm not interested in."

"Molly, I don't want you to get the wrong impression. I didn't come to California to find romance. Not at my age. I came to relieve some of the guilt that's on Leland's mind and to make sure my daughter's getting along all right. And I'm going back home to the life I left there."

But Molly sat thinking for a long time while her mother was getting dressed. Now that both Leland and her mother were widowed, perhaps they could enjoy each other's company more freely. It was an intriguing notion, and one that brought a contemplative smile to her face.

Molly took a long time to dress after her mother left the apartment. Mr. Gunther had brought all her things, carefully packed by his housekeeper, when he'd come to dinner last night, and she already felt quite at home in her new surroundings, even though she was always aware that she was living in a building owned by Brett Sterling.

When Molly came down to the lobby, she involuntarily gave a look of dread toward the special penthouse elevator nearby. But instead of Brett, she saw a striking blond couple waiting, both leaning on one foot in almost identically juvenile poses. Chuck Yancey and his sister Rita were waiting to go up to the penthouse.

Before she could slip quietly past them, Chuck turned and saw her.

"Molly! What are you doing here?" Chuck said, and Rita gave a start as she recognized Molly.

"I've taken an apartment here for awhile with my mother. Sort of a vacation, you might say."

"I believe you've met my sister Rita, haven't you?"

"Yes, how are—"

"How do you do," Rita said as if they had never before laid eyes on one another.

Chuck seemed pleased to have a sudden inspiration. "I'm glad we ran into you. I'm on my way up to discuss some boat deals with Brett, and Rita always gets mad when we get into one of these boring discussions. Why don't you two get better acquainted? Have lunch together."

Rita looked almost as unenthusiastic about Chuck's idea as Molly until her brother pulled a twenty dollar bill from his pocket and pressed it into her hand.

"Here, my treat. Thanks to Molly, I got paid for crewing yesterday when I was supposed to be on vacation."

The girls left the building together as if they had just been consigned to a forced march. Molly tried to find some common ground for conversation as they made their way over to the outdoor patio of the convivial restaurant in the nearby shopping center.

"Chuck told me that you're both newcomers to California," she said. "How do you like it?"

The girl's sullen face suddenly lit up.

"Oh, I love it. There's so much excitement, especially here at the marina. Everyone's always leaving to go someplace, or do something fun." Molly had trouble keeping up with Rita's mercurial mood swings.

"Sounds as though you love to travel."

"Oh, I do. That's why I'm so glad I found Brett. He's always planning some trip or sending us off somewhere to pick up a boat for him." Her voice rose and fell with unbridled enthusiasm.

They had no trouble finding a table as it was still early in the lunch hour. They settled down under a bright umbrella near the sidewalk entrance. Rita seemed more content now that she had people to look at, and something besides Molly to respond to.

"Do you want a glass of wine?" Rita asked.

"That might be nice," Molly answered.

"We'll have a bottle of your white wine," Rita told the waitress. Somehow the glass of wine had grown to an entire bottle before Molly could stop her.

"Are you old enough to order wine?" Molly asked.

"I happen to be twenty-four years old, and I've been making my own decisions for a long time now," Rita said. Apparently she sensed that Molly had been about to change the order, so she spoke with stubborn authority.

Molly studied the girl carefully. She realized that the girl could be her own age. She was delicate, with pale white skin protected from the sun by a layer of pancake makeup and a wide-brimmed hat. It was the lithe youthfulness of her body that made her seem adolescent.

"You see, I talked my brother into taking off with me to see the world. We had to beg money wherever we could, bed down any old place. Oh, it was so much fun! Really romantic, never knowing where we'd be the next day."

Molly remembered that Chuck's account of their years as runaways had been very different. Apparently he had found only uncertainty and peril in the footloose life his older sister had dragged him reluctantly into.

"Then how did you finally end up here?" Molly asked, indicating with a gesture that she meant the entire marina, when in fact her curiosity was more confined to how Rita had wound up in Brett Sterling's penthouse.

"Well, Chuck kind of took to sailing, and it was just lucky for me that he went to work for Brett when we got here."

When the wine came, Rita poured herself a full glass and drank it down before Molly had an opportunity to pour herself any.

"Now I have everything I want," Rita continued. "We can sail off whenever things get too dull. Mmmm, this wine is good. Did you know we're planning a trip to Tahiti? We're going to cruise all over the South Pacific."

Molly took one tiny sip of wine to every thirsty gulp of Rita's. She studied the red and white stripes of the tablecloth with her fingernail as she glumly considered how self-satisfied Rita was to have snagged herself the rich and fun-loving man in the penthouse. It was probably an ideal match, she told herself sourly.

Molly called the waitress over with a nod, but Rita wasn't ready to order any food as yet, so the waitress left them to their wine. As Rita drank more wine, she grew more gregarious, her pale cheeks flushed as she gestured expansively, toasting the many trips to faraway places that she had planned for herself.

"What about Chuck? What does he want to do with his life?" Molly asked.

"Oh, he's a stick-in-the-mud. He just wants to stay right here and design boats and build boats and repair boats and then watch them sail away. And Brett will back him all the way. He's already promised me that." She grabbed at her glass so impulsively that she almost tipped it over.

Brett's already promised her a lot, Molly thought bitterly. But did the girl realize that he might be fickle with his promises? When another willing young thing came along, he would probably not hesitate to move on to a new liaison. For all her world-wise talk, Rita was just as naive and vulnerable as the most sheltered New England girl with her nose in a book, and just as sensitive to pain and disappointment at the hands of a ruthless womanizer like Brett Sterling. Brett was incapable of really caring about any woman. Rita did not realize that, and she would doubtless be destroyed by the man. But Molly was determined that she would not let that happen to herself. She was going to wash her mind of him the way the waves of a high tide clean the beach. She would force herself to be impervious to the dynamic force of his personality, she thought resolutely.

Brett was suddenly standing beside her, as if she had magically conjured him up by merely thinking of him, and she jumped slightly as he rasped at Rita, "I can see Molly Weston has been a bad influence on you."

Though the words he spoke could have been in jest, there was no trace of humor in his delivery.

"Why, Brett," Rita answered him demurely. "How nice you've come to join us. We're just having a glass of wine."

"Was that your idea?" he said to Molly.

"Chuck suggested we have lunch together," Molly said.

"Yes, he told me you were having lunch, but I don't see any food on the table."

"We're just about to order," Molly stammered, wondering why she had been put so quickly on trial, while Rita seemed unconcerned.

Brett pulled a chair from an unoccupied table near them and sat down. After his loud, accusatory tone with Molly, he now lowered his voice gently as he spoke to Rita.

"You've been told you're not to drink anything. And this bottle is almost empty."

"Molly likes wine with her meal. We were sharing it," Rita said, her blue eyes wide and guileless.

Molly's first glass of wine still stood in front of her barely touched. This willful girl who could never be influenced to do anything she didn't want to, was only confirming Brett's suspicion that she'd been led astray by Molly's bad habits. And Brett was always ready to think the worst of Molly. It was all too much, and Molly started to stand up to leave.

"Just a minute, I want to talk to you," Brett's hand closed over her wrist, wrenching her painfully back into her chair. Again his voice changed tone. "Rita, you get over to the dock and see if you can help Mac clean up that boat. I'll talk to you about this tonight."

Rita leaned down to kiss Brett's cheek, her hands brushing about his neck so seductively that Molly looked up to study the billowing cloud formations in the sky with more interest than usual.

"I'm all right, Brett, really I am," Rita assured him, effectively neutralizing his anger with either her words or her adroit fingers.

"I know you are, and I'm sorry to sound so strict. But believe me, it's for your own good. It's only because I care about you," Brett spoke slowly to the girl.

Rita left them, her graceful hip movements drawing interested spectator glances toward her tight jeans as she strolled out of the patio.

"I don't want that girl drinking a drop of liquor," Brett said with renewed strictness.

"I'm sorry. I didn't realize she had a problem."

"She doesn't have any problem. It's just that she's a nervous and excitable girl; I'm sure you must have noticed that. And I want her to learn to face life without any artificial stimulation. She doesn't need any, she's lively enough."

"I'd certainly have to agree she's lively. But do you think she needs so much protection against her evil drinking companions? She seems to me to be a grown-up girl with a mind of her own. She's no younger than I am, you know."

"And of course we know you're quite able to make your own decisions, without anyone's advice," he said sarcastically.

"You mean your so-called advice that I leave Mr. Gunther's employment?"

"Employment, or whatever you like to call it."

"Is that what you kept me here to talk about?"

"No, I'm through giving you advice about your reputation, or lack of it. All I want to know is whether Mr. Gunther wants that boat or not."

"He has his mind on other things right now. I don't think he's given any more thought to the boat purchase."

Brett moved the glasses and bottle around on the table as if he wanted to throw them all on the floor. Then he stopped mid-motion to look at Molly through wickedly narrowed eyes. "Is this your way of getting even with me? Just because I discovered the truth behind your self-righteous pose, I suppose you told him to forget all about buying you the boat."

"He wasn't buying the boat for me, I've tried to tell you that. It was for himself. And he makes his own decisions. But he seems to have other diversions on his mind right now."

"I've heard all about the love nest," Brett spat out the words with derision.

"The *what?*"

"My leasing agent told me how thrilled your Mr. Gunther was to sign up our last available apartment for you."

"That apartment is for my mother. He sent her a plane ticket so she could come out and visit me. That was the surprise he had waiting for me last night."

"Well, your mother will lend your little arrangement just the right touch of respectability. Mr. Gunther need not worry that any of his important business friends will suspect him of his secret vice. What a hypocrite!"

"I'm sick of your mudslinging. You don't know what you're talking about."

"Then let's stick to business. I brought that boat

up here for Mr. Gunther to see. Then he didn't even bother to show up for his test cruise. And now you tell me he's found other playthings more amusing than a yacht."

"Certainly you don't succeed at every deal you set out to make. There must have been someone else, somewhere, who said no to what you had to offer. And you'll just have to resign yourself to it this time."

Brett gave her a crooked smile in recognition of the fact that she was now the one indulging in double entendres. She felt the need to hurt him by reminding him that not only had Mr. Gunther turned down the boat, but she had also turned down Brett's lovemaking on that memorable first night at Catalina. But Brett's ego was impenetrable.

"I'm not ready to give up yet," he said. "When you've got a good product to sell, you just sit back and wait and it sells itself." He leaned back in his chair as if he planned to do the waiting right here at the restaurant, amusement flickering in his blue eyes.

"Mr. Gunther doesn't need a boat right now. With my mother here he'll be too busy to think about it."

"Then why did he call me this morning with more questions? You see, we still have unfinished business. Now, what I want to know is whether to keep the *Princess* here or return it to its home port. I can only hold this particular boat for him a little while longer."

Molly felt a pang of loss as she thought of that beautiful red ketch being sold to someone else.

"Do whatever you want. I can't advise you," she snapped.

Brett stood up to leave, but not without leaving

her with a touch as gentle as a breeze to remember.
He trailed his hand across her back as he leaned over
to apologize.

"I'm sorry I came down on you so hard about the
wine. I worry about Rita, probably more than I
should. But I can't help it. She needs a good firm
hand, and, thank God, she's found one."

Then the hand on her back tensed, his thoughts
obviously now completely absorbed by his concern
for Rita. And moments after she'd lost his attention,
she lost him entirely, for without a word of farewell
he disappeared toward the crowded parking lot
where he'd presumably left his car.

He'd never thought to offer her a ride back to the
tower. In fact he'd never thought about her in any
way but as an object of his criticism. The care he
lavished on Rita was apparently hers alone to enjoy.

But she had been wrong about Brett in one
respect, and now she had to admit it to herself. He
did have the capacity to care deeply for someone.
He'd shown that with his furrowed brow and his
concentration on Rita's problems.

Molly would never have believed that he could
feel so passionately involved with someone. Chuck
had tried to tell her of Brett's kindness and his
generosity toward the two homeless waifs. But now
she knew that it went much further than that.
Apparently he felt that Rita deserved special protection to keep her life on an even keel. He seemed to
ignore the fact that this childlike little blonde had for
several years bummed around the country with a
reluctant younger brother in tow, surviving the
rigorous challenges of life on the road and arriving at
exactly the point where she wanted to be.

"Are you going to order anything, or is this it?"

The waitress nodded toward the empty wine bottle, and for the second time that day Molly was made

to feel like a dissolute lunch hour drinker. What's more, she was going to have to pay for that bottle she had barely tasted, for Rita and Brett had both abandoned her without a thought about paying for it.

"Bring me a cheeseburger with everything on it," she said with sudden determination.

She had left her apartment that morning for lunch alone in the sun. The Zane Grey novel that she'd bought in Catalina was in her purse so that she'd have something to amuse herself with. Now she was going to go ahead with that plan. But, she wondered, as she opened the book, if everything had worked out just as she'd envisioned, why was she feeling so sorry for herself as she sat alone and forgotten in the busy cafe?

Chapter Seven

"Now is that any way to spend your vacation?" Charlotte asked her daughter.

For two days Molly had stayed snuggled on the couch with a stack of books and a box of graham crackers, her hair uncombed, her face ghostly for want of the touch of a lipstick brush.

"You are either going to come along with Leland and me to the museum today, or you're going to think up something more interesting for yourself," her mother warned sternly. "All this moping about is doing you no good."

Molly stood up and stretched, knowing that her mother was right.

"I'll go sailing, that's what I'll do. I saw a place that rents small sailboats, and I'll take one out. There's a good wind today."

"Now that's more like the daughter I remember."

As Molly put on a pair of navy cords and a French sailor's striped cotton pullover, she felt the enticing potential for adventure that any sailing trip offered. She pulled her hair into a clump at the back of her neck, then tied a bright red scarf around it for some color, and walked out the door and down the hall toward the elevator. She was moving away from her saddened spirit as fast as she could, putting as much space as possible between herself and her thoughts about Brett Sterling.

By the time she arrived at the tiny office on the boat rental dock she had outrun all the demons that were pursuing her, so that she must have appeared cheerful enough for the attendant to say with confidence, "You look like you can handle a Lido 14. Sign here."

The man pointed out the one assigned to her and Molly went down the dock toward it. On each side of her were long rows of fluttering white sails, the boats waiting like birds warming their wings, anxious to be rented for takeoff. She tossed her big canvas tote bag into the boat.

It took her awhile to adjust to the tricky turns of the wind. She hadn't sailed a boat this size in many years, but before long she was tacking back and forth across the harbor, zigzagging her course to keep the wind always across her bow. She had no destination in mind so she let the winds lead her, and she explored areas of the harbor she'd never seen before.

There was little boat traffic around her, for it was a weekday and too early in the afternoon for the day trip sailors to be returning. An occasional sailboat would pass her and she'd watch the crew scurrying about, remembering her last sail. She found herself comparing every boat she saw with either the *Princess* or the *Pleasure Seeker*. And she imagined that the captain behind every wheel was Brett Sterling.

During the few days she'd been away from him

she'd had the time to think, and she had come to the reluctant decision that she was in love with him. It was not the kind of love she had ever expected to experience. She had always dreamed of finding a man from her own hometown, a man who would offer her a quiet life, be a good father and an attentive husband. She was sorry now that she had come to California and forsaken any chances of finding a binding love like that. Instead she was wasting her time in hopeless pursuit of dreams.

She and Brett were undeniably attracted to each other, yet neither had a shred of respect for the other. Their relationship was doomed, and she knew it, and now she must simply fill her days with constructive pursuits until the pain ebbed and she was able to face her empty life.

No man would ever be able to enthrall her with such tormenting feelings of desire, and she was sure no other man would ever have such ability to hurt her. Whatever pale imitation of this love she some-day found, it would be less wearing on her, less destructive, than her violently ambivalent feelings toward Brett.

She had another hour before the sun would be setting, so she decided to sail out into the main channel, down the long low rock pile of the jetty, which was the marina's main boulevard to the ocean.

She noticed a motorboat heading into her path, but she knew the rules of the sea commanded that a powerboat give a sailing craft the right-of-way, so she waited for him to turn and avoid her. But the young boy managing the boat, on his way home from a day of water skiing, was busy laughing and talking with his passengers, and didn't appear interested in boat etiquette. As he hurtled toward her path, it became obvious he didn't see her, so Molly pushed the tiller away from her and let go of the sheet, throwing her little boat into confusion, but stopping its forward motion.

"Hey, watch where you're going," the boy called from the other boat.

He had finally noticed her and stopped his boat with a cloud of exhaust fumes just inches from Molly. She was drifting helplessly toward the side of his boat, with no way to propel herself away from him now that she'd sacrificed all the wind in her sails in order to stop. The boy leaned over to grab hold of her sail.

"You'll scratch my boat. Keep away!" he called.

"Please don't hold onto my sail. I need to catch the wind. If you don't let go, I'll tip over," she pleaded.

Molly felt the boat beneath her give an ominous shudder as it responded to a gust of wind while trapped in the rude stranger's hold. Then she felt the boat slowly tip beyond the point of no return, almost as if it were going in slow motion, and then she felt a rush of cold water.

Suddenly everything was deathly still, and Molly was seeing an eerie world through a green filter. She realized she was underwater, but she was not frightened. She knew she would quickly bob to the surface, for her years of training had taught her to fall far so that she would not be trapped beneath the boat. With a gush of bubbles she popped up into the more familiar world.

"You people in sailboats ought to be more careful," the boy called, gunning his motor to speed his party on its way.

Molly moved her arms slowly to hold herself up in the water as she looked at her forlorn Lido 14, floating on its side nearby with no intention of sinking. The mast was now horizontal, still supporting the single sail, which was resting full of water like a man's dress shirt put to soak in a laundry tub. She decided to try to rock the boat upright by swimming around to where the exposed keel was sticking up into the air.

She hoisted herself up, her arms straining to push down on the protruding starboard deck, throwing all her weight into the rocking motion with which she hoped to pop the boat out of the water. It was strenuous work, and it was a long time before she began to see the mast quiver as it tried to bring itself vertical again. But the weight of dragging the wet sail with it out of the water seemed too much. With a tired sigh, Molly decided to swim and tow the boat closer to the rocks, and then go to work removing the mast, a tricky procedure from her position in the water, which she didn't look forward to.

"Oh, that's the funniest thing I've ever seen! Who ever heard of towing a sailboat? Wasn't it going fast enough for you?"

Molly couldn't believe her ears, but she was almost certain that the malicious laughter and the taunting comments came from her least favorite lunchtime companion, Rita Yancey. She put her dog paddle into reverse, then looked over her shoulder to see a large black form looming over her. From her low viewpoint in the water it seemed like an ominous storm cloud. Actually, it was the darkly-painted hull of a sloop and it had come up behind her so noiselessly that she hadn't been aware of it. Rita was leaning over the side as it slid past Molly in the water. Then when the stern came into her view, Molly was chagrined to see the familiar lettering spelling out *Pleasure Seeker* across the transom.

Brett Sterling was behind the wheel of his boat, and he was putting down a pair of binoculars, so apparently he'd been observing her plight from afar for quite a while. Now he called out to her in an exasperated tone. "Why aren't you wearing a life jacket? Get out of the water and onto the rocks immediately!"

Molly was so tired that she was glad to let someone else take charge of the reclamation project, and she did as she was told.

Brett was busy lowering a swim ladder that folded out of the pulpit, and at the same time brought his boat to an unsteady stop.

"Are you rested enough to swim over here?" he called to her.

Sitting drenched and bedraggled on the rocks, she realized just how exhausted she was, but his welcome decks were only a few yards away and she nodded her head, took a couple of relaxing deep breaths, and then waded back into the water and swam toward him, clumsy in her heavy wet corduroy pants.

As Brett helped her up the ladder, she noticed he was staring at her with an amused grin. She realized what a picture she must be, her hair soaked, and her clothes clinging to her. He made no secret of his interest as she tried to pull loose the T-shirt, which was now plastered to her body. She couldn't help but wish that she'd worn a bra beneath it so that his investigative glance wouldn't have been rewarded with such a revealing look at her.

Rita was still laughing to herself as she made her way to the stern to get closer to Molly's disgrace. "I thought you were supposed to be seaworthy. Brett told us you knew something about sailing," she said.

"A motorboat came by and it wouldn't yield the right-of-way," Molly gasped as she tried to catch her breath. "Then he grabbed hold of my sail and when a gust of wind came along, I flipped right over."

"Did you ask them to stay and help you, or go for the Harbor Patrol?" Brett asked, implying that she hadn't kept her head during the emergency.

"I can take care of everything by myself," she said with defiance.

"Oh, sure, we can see that!" the frisky girl in the trim white bikini said to her mockingly. Rita was obviously enjoying herself immensely; her hands fluttering to hold her huge straw sun hat in place were too busy to offer Molly a towel.

"I wonder if you have another swimsuit I could borrow," Molly asked. "In these clothes I can't get around in the water very well."

"When you're out in a boat that size, you should always wear a bathing suit under your clothes," Brett said.

"And I should wear my life jacket, and I should send for the Harbor Patrol," she snapped back. "I guess I didn't do anything right."

"I'm glad I came along to save you," Brett said, playing the hero to the hilt, and relishing the role. "Rita, since you're dressed for swimming, you jump in and see if you can right the boat."

"Brett, that water's freezing," she protested immediately.

"Is that swimsuit merely decorative, or do you wear it for a reason?" he asked her, spacing his words.

"But I'll wash off all my suntan oil," she said.

Brett reached over and took the hat off of her head and then gave her a playful spank on her almost nonexistent behind. "A little bit of sun won't hurt you, and it won't hurt you to help out a friend in need either."

"If you insist," Rita grumbled, making it clear she was making the sacrifice for Brett, not on the basis of any friendship for Molly.

Rita didn't waste time climbing down the ladder. In one quick motion she leaped onto the deck and dove into the water, barely causing a ripple as her taut body slipped into a tiny crease in the water.

Molly sat shivering as she watched Rita flip the boat back up with one or two energetic bounces. She had amazing strength for one so slight. As she swam back, her white body side-stroking through the water like a sleek moray eel, she held Molly's tote bag aloft and dragged a life jacket behind her.

"You keep the jacket and put it on," Brett told her as he leaned over to take Molly's purse.

"Why do I need it?" Rita asked, grabbing hold of the ladder in the water.

"Because you're going to sail Molly's boat back to the rental dock."

"But Brett, what about our picnic? We have so much to talk about, and this was our chance to be alone."

"There will be plenty of time for picnics, now show off what a good little boater you are," Brett cajoled winningly.

"This isn't fair! Just because Molly doesn't know how to sail, I have to take back a boat with a sail full of salt water."

"You can wind that man at the rental dock around your little finger. Now go on and do me this favor. I'll make it up to you, you know that."

"You owe me one, Brett Sterling," she said as she began her slow backstroke away from him, lifting each arm as suggestively as if she were inviting his embrace.

"And knowing you, I'll pay," he laughed with gentle amusement as he watched her reluctantly go to do his bidding.

Brett had apparently forgotten Molly's presence, as he always did when Rita was around. He hovered

over the side of his boat with concern as he watched
the girl climb into the Lido, bail out the water in it
and take control of the sail. He didn't look back
toward Molly until he was sure Rita was safely on
her way.

"You should have let me take that boat back," she
said. "You and Rita obviously had plans, and I've
interrupted them."

"You are in no condition to sail that boat. Look at
you."

Molly realized what a pathetic sight she must be.
The scarf which had held her hair was now dripping
red dye onto her shirt, her hair was drying, matted,
around her face, and her pants contained pounds of
moisture.

"I could have handled the situation." She had
worked hard to win his faint praise of her nautical
skills, and now right in front of him she had suffered
a disaster. And to make things worse, he hadn't
thought she had the presence of mind to work her
way out of it. She shivered slightly, her pride utterly
deflated.

"The sun will be going down soon and you'll catch
cold. Go below and get out of those things," he said.

"Just drop me off at the nearest dock," she asked,
not wishing to spend any more time with him in her
current dejected state.

"I had planned a sunset picnic right outside the
breakwater. It looks as though it's going to be a
beautiful evening and I don't have any intention of
changing my plans."

Molly shrugged her shoulders, knowing how use-
less it was to argue with him when he'd made up his
mind about something. She headed for the companionway.

"Here, you can wrap up in this." He tossed her a
big beach towel, which landed almost on top of her.

She went to Brett's luxurious cabin and stripped out of her wet clothes immediately, glad to be rid of their clammy chill. Just as she was standing wondering what to do next, she heard a hand jiggle the doorknob. She grabbed up the towel he'd given her, and wrapped it hastily around her.

"What do you want?" she asked shakily.

"Your wet clothes. I'll hang them on the lifeline to dry."

She opened the door a few inches and handed him her clothes, but he pushed it open further, and tossing the clothes behind him, he stepped inside. She reached up to untie the dripping scarf and handed it to him. But he threw that behind him, too, and stood mutely watching her as she shook her hair loose.

"What would Mr. Leland Gunther say if he could see us now?" he said, wetting his sunburned lips with a swipe of his tongue.

"I don't know—I mean, he couldn't care less, I'm sure."

"Here you are almost naked beside my berth, and you say he doesn't care?" He spoke the words with an unmistakable light of desire in his eyes. "Well, then, what's stopping us?"

He reached for her, taking her into his arms heedless of her precarious hold on the towel wrapped around her. She clung to it so that her arms were painfully crushed against her chest as he enfolded her.

He whispered into her ear. "I've been waiting to catch you like this since the first day I showed you this cabin."

He pushed her backward so that her bare legs brushed the luxury of the fur throw on his bed. The dim afternoon sun was casting a slanted beam through the clear hatch over Brett's head. The light seemed to set his hair afire, and it turned his eyes to blazing aquamarine.

"Brett, please don't do this—" she began. But she was in love with him, how could she expect to reject his touch forever, even knowing how little he cared for her?

"I'm going to kiss every freckle on your body," he smiled at her. "Even if it takes me until tomorrow."

She closed her eyes and relived all the recent sensations of falling overboard into the water. First there was that drop through time and space while waiting for the inevitable to happen. Then the dizzying feeling of being disoriented in an environment where a heavy pressure pushed on her from all sides. Then the desperate struggle to save herself. But this time she was not so lucky. She could feel her resistance to him sinking like a stone in the water's depths.

"You don't know what you're doing to me," she said with a tortured cry, the skin on her face burning under his lips as he began his promised tour.

"I know exactly what I'm doing," he said between kisses.

His voice was strong with hints of the delights he had in store for her. She knew she should push him away from her now while she still could, but when she reached up to touch his shoulders, she felt the towel begin to slip, so she pulled herself closer to him to protect herself.

Feeling what he thought was a positive response from her, Brett moved the length of his body closer to hers, and she let herself ripple against him. The twisting motions of their bodies pressing together slowly worked the towel down until Molly felt it descend like a cloud onto her feet. Her breasts, now bare, were stroked by the folds of his terry cloth shirt.

She trembled, and would have swayed from his arms to pitch onto the floor in a heap with the towel had he not kept her prisoner in his arms.

"This is where you belong, Molly," Brett said in a husky whisper close to her ear. Then between words his trail of kisses led him down her neck toward her shoulders. "Let me prove it, let me convince you—Oh, Blast!"

He pulled away from her sharply, and threw himself toward the berth. Resting on one knee, he leaned over to look through the stained-glass porthole. "You've made me forget where I am!"

Molly pulled her wrapping back up into place, glad his attention was so diverted that he hadn't noticed the lapse in modesty. He had indeed made her forget where she was or what she was doing.

"We're going to drift right onto those rocks if I don't do something in a hurry." He started to leave the cabin. "Stay right where you are."

He turned to kiss her quickly, the brightness in his eyes undiminished in spite of the sudden distraction, and then disappeared, mumbling dire threats and oaths at his beloved boat as he strode through her small salon in three or four steps.

Molly sat down on his berth, but her mind followed right behind Brett, reaching for him and pulling at him with all of her senses. She sat in a daze, feeling the reaction of the boat as Brett began putting it once again under control. She knew he would drop anchor in the ocean and soon he would be back here with her, weaving his special spell over her. The sunlight cascaded through the bright panels of stained glass, matching the hallucinatory nature of her thoughts as she dreamed on.

When the towel began to slip again, she let it. Sitting nude upon Brett's bed she felt as alien as if she were an actor in a play, and she didn't care for the drama she'd been cast in.

This is just what he had planned for this afternoon, she thought. A romantic sunset picnic, uninterrupted while at sea. It didn't matter to him who shared the feast. It had been planned for Rita, but when Rita had been sidetracked, no matter. He had quickly replaced her with someone else. With anyone. With Molly.

He thought of her as a wanton, able to turn on passionate abandon for a man whenever it was to her advantage. That was why he had thought her an easy replacement.

She fastened the towel securely around herself and jumped up to go to the companionway and call out to him harshly, "Don't you keep any extra clothes on this luxury liner?" feeling again like a half-drowned victim of a shipwreck.

"Who needs clothes?" he smiled back at her.

"I want to get dressed. I'm cold."

He was in the sunlight, and she knew he couldn't see her face in the shadows below, but apparently he caught her meaning from the tone of her voice because his answer was subdued and deliberate when it came.

"Rita keeps some things in a locker."

"I suspected she might."

"Try that first one on the port side."

Molly opened the latch and out tumbled several hats. Apparently Rita liked to keep a variety on board so that she could keep her fair skin protected at all times. On a top shelf in the locker there was a jumble of beauty aids, but most of them were sun lotions. Brett was used to her careful ways, that's why he was always criticizing Molly for not taking more care. She knew that right now her face was shiny and pink from the day's exposure. He probably thought her terribly unsophisticated compared to the more beauty-conscious Rita.

She unrolled a shirt that seemed less wrinkled than the rest, and found a pair of wadded-up shorts that looked as if they might fit her, and quickly dressed, anxious to get above deck and out of the cabin area where she felt so vulnerable.

When Brett saw her coming on deck, he gave her wardrobe a close look and a scowl of disapproval, but didn't mention it. "Why don't you bring the picnic basket with you? I think I've found a spot to anchor. Oh, and there's a bottle of champagne chilling."

"I don't want any."

"I see the winds have shifted," he said, wrinkling his forehead as he looked at her. "I detect a chill wind from the north."

"That's right," she said, and she went below to fetch the basket and two cold soft drink cans.

She was rather surprised that Brett had accepted her change in attitude so complacently. Of course, he was now too occupied with navigating the boat to press the issue. But maybe he wasn't really interested in continuing what they'd started.

Brett's timing, as usual, was faultless. He had planned a sunset picnic, and at the moment the hamper was opened the sun disappeared over the horizon, leaving a fanfare of bright pinks and reds in the sky.

Molly watched as Brett pulled out cheeses and pâtés and cold salmon spread with mustard sauce. She opened the box of water biscuits and they began to eat.

"Orange drink doesn't really go with this," he complained.

"You had planned a very elegant supper," she said, ignoring his desire for the ignored bottle below.

"My chef at the Sterling Towers likes to impress me. He's quite outdone himself this time. And he'd picked out a very nice imported champagne to go with it."

Molly choked on a sip of the carbonated drink. Its harsh taste did not complement the meal, but she was determined not to give in to his self-pitying hints about how she was ruining his gourmet plans.

"You can save the champagne for a more appropriate occasion. Like the next time you get Rita on board alone," she said, her voice as iced as the bottle that so dominated their conversation.

"She wanted this time alone because we needed to talk. Usually Mac or Chuck are around."

"Well, perhaps you can share it when you have something to celebrate," she said, toasting him with her drink can.

"I was hoping to have something to celebrate tonight," he said, too distracted by his thoughts of Rita to let her antagonism bother him.

"I'm sure you were."

"She has a decision to make, and the champagne was to celebrate if she made the right choice. Sometimes I have to push the girl a bit to make her do what she knows she should do."

"I'm sure your advice and counsel are irresistible to her."

"I hope so," he said, his head lowered thoughtfully so that his high cheekbones caught the orange glow of the spectacular sunset.

"I'm sorry I came along and spoiled your plans. It's too bad Rita missed this," she said. She regretted at once her words, for they were spoken in spite, and now he would get the impression that she was jealous of Rita. But she could think of no way to explain to him that it was his whole easy attitude toward women that repelled her. At the moment it was Rita who stood between them, but it could be someone else just as well. He could never be a one-woman man, and she could never settle for a relationship with a philanderer, no matter how much she loved him. The differences between them were tremendous and irreconcilable, no matter how strongly they felt the physical pull of their yearnings for one another. Chuck had said Brett's father chased after women, and apparently he had inherited the tendencies.

He spread a cracker thickly with peppered Boursin cheese, but held it in midair to stare at her speculatively. She couldn't be sure if he was concentrating on her, or wishing he could exchange her for the company of the more cooperative Rita.

"I'm going away for awhile," he said suddenly.

"Oh, are you? Is it a business trip?"

"No. I'm going to sail down the coast of Baja California."

"Sounds like an interesting trip. How lucky you are that you can afford the time for such excursions."

"I need to get away, so I'll make the time. When I get back, things will be different." His sigh was one of resignation.

They talked very little as they finished off the contents of the picnic basket. Both were lost in their own thoughts. Brett's were as unfathomable to her as always, but her own were repetitions of the same old refrain that had circled her mind since morning. All she could think about was the utter hopelessness of loving such a man.

After they finished eating, Brett gathered up the remnants of the meal and took them below. He brought up two bulky float coats with him for them to wear on the trip home, for it was now almost dark. With the absence of the sun the winds would be cold. He put on his own and then held the extra jacket for her to slip into. After she'd put her arms into the sleeves he turned her gently toward him and zipped the front for her as if she were a helpless child. She let him do it, relaxing to enjoy the fleeting moment of feeling protected and cherished by him. Such moments were rare, and she wanted to appreciate them now, and have them to remember. He put his arms around her, holding her loosely, for the bulky jackets they were wearing made any embrace seem like the attempt of two snowmen to get close.

"Will you miss me?"

"I'm sure many people will," she said, knowing that each day she didn't see him would be empty for her.

"Perhaps if things had worked out differently a little while ago, I wouldn't have been able to go."

"What do you mean?" she asked, genuinely mystified by his words.

"Don't act dense. You know what I mean. If you hadn't been in such a hurry to find those clothes."

Molly remembered what Chuck had told her that day when they were sailing back from Catalina. He said that whenever Brett had a problem he couldn't solve, or something on his mind which was troubling him, he sailed off on an adventure to give himself time to think.

"Why exactly did you plan this cruise to Baja?" she asked.

Brett dropped his arms from their hold on her so abruptly that she felt as if her float coat had been deflated.

She continued, "Are you trying to escape from something? What are you running away from?"

"From you," he answered simply.

His answer shocked her. She had never realized how thwarted he felt by her rejections of his lovemaking. Apparently she was one woman who wouldn't give him what he wanted, and he found her attitude even more baffling because he believed she was available for Leland Gunther and yet holding herself aloof from him. He obviously felt she was the ultimate challenge, and when she wouldn't give in to him, he planned to sail away and forget her for good.

"I wish you bon voyage," she said. Without acknowledging her, he went forward to raise the anchor so that they could return to the marina. They had once again reached the point of impasse.

As they pulled into Brett's slip at the Sterling Anchorage, Molly felt like a leaky scow being tugged back to port. She went below to change back into her own clothes. They were still damp and stiff from their saltwater soaking, but she wanted to return Rita's things to the locker right now so she wouldn't have to see her again.

As she changed she noticed for the first time a cardboard box full of miscellaneous items that had recently been brought on board. It was sitting next to Rita's locker as if the girl had been in the process of unpacking it when Molly's sailboat had been spotted overturned near the rocks. In the box were several bottles of wine, a backgammon set, a deck of cards and several bright flashes of shimmery fabric that indicated the girl wanted several extra bikinis on board.

Now Molly knew that the girl had been invited to accompany Brett on his getaway cruise. That would be Brett's idea of a perfect solution to his dilemma. He could easily put to rest his improbable passion for Molly with Rita along to help him forget. He had brought Rita with him today to invite her, and she had, of course, come prepared to accept. All that had been lacking was the champagne celebration, which Molly had spoiled by her appearance on the scene.

When she went up to disembark, Brett was already off the boat, waiting on the dock with her tote bag in hand.

"Don't forget your portable library," he said, and he laughed at her as he fingered the damp books in her bag. "I'm surprised you didn't pull one out to read while we were having our picnic."

"I'm not much fun to have along on a cruise," she sniffed, starting away.

"That's not what Leland Gunther would say, I'm sure," he called after her as a parting shot as she headed up the gangplank into the darkness.

Chapter Eight

The next morning Molly was up and dressed long before her mother had awakened. She left a note for her, and then went to her car and headed for the freeway. She was halfway to Mr. Gunther's house before she remembered that she'd forgotten breakfast. A few blocks from Mr. Gunther's house there was a donut shop, and she stopped to pick up two maple crullers and cup of coffee to go. Today she was not going to count calories, she was going to spoil herself by doing exactly what she wanted.

Given the freedom to do what pleased her today, she had decided to get back to work. Despite her mother's warning that Leland didn't want her back at the office, she was going to busy herself with the routines and procedures that would comfort her. She was going to eat her breakfast with one hand, fill in the ledger books with the other, and have a phone to her ear hearing stock quotes at the same time, she planned, so that she would be too busy to think about the debacle that her mother and Leland had called her "vacation time."

She used her special key to let herself in the outside entrance to the library at Mr. Gunther's house where their office was located. As soon as she stepped inside she realized that she had forgotten her old routines. Her first act upon opening the door should have been to disconnect the burglar alarm, and now she had only a few seconds left in which to disengage it or a loud alarm would roar throughout the house and simultaneously summon the police on a special telephone line. She dropped her purse and grabbed for the disconnecting switch, but at that moment the lid popped off the coffee container and she cried out as the hot liquid burned her hands. The clamorous alarm soon drowned out her moan.

Before long she was standing at her desk explaining herself to Leland; Perkins, the chauffeur; and the housekeeper. Luckily she'd called the police and stopped them before they had sent a squad car.

"So our sneak thief turned out to be Molly sneaking in to work," Leland chuckled. "Well, go back to bed, Mrs. Okimoto, and get back to reading the paper, Perkins. Molly is going to share her bag of donuts with me and explain herself."

"Leland, I'm so sorry I awakened you. I just can't seem to do anything right, anymore."

"I was awake, honey. I heard your car drive in and I was going to come down and find out what you were doing here at this hour. Aren't you supposed to be keeping your mother company?"

"You seem to be doing a good job of that all by yourself," she said. "Right now I need to work. So let me get at it." She sat down to rifle through a stack of unopened mail.

"I could use your help today, I suppose," Leland

said. "I'm having a little dinner party here tonight.
It's nothing fancy, just dinner for four. But I want it
to be very special. You and your mother are to be
here in your prettiest finery at eight o'clock."

"You said dinner for four. Who else is coming?"

"I didn't know who to invite as your dinner
partner, so I called Brett Sterling. I feel kind of bad
about losing interest in the boat project right in the
middle of all his efforts."

"Oh, no. Have you already invited him?" Molly
said, the letter in her hand trembling slightly as she
prayed she could intercept the invitation.

"Talked to him on the phone yesterday morning."

Molly stood up to walk toward the coffee tray
hoping her suddenly weakened knees would support
her. "He didn't say anything about this last night."

"You were with him last night?" Leland asked,
smiling as if he'd stumbled upon a more promising
twosome for his dinner party than he had imagined.
"I didn't know you were keeping company with the
young man."

"I'm not keeping company with him. It happened
quite by accident. I was out sailing and I happened
to have a little trouble with my boat and he—he
helped me, that's all."

"He'd be a mighty fine person to have around in
time of trouble, I can tell that about the fellow."

"I think he's haughty, and arrogant, and he's been
very rude every time he's talked to you. I don't
know how you can stand him," she blurted out,
happy to be able to put into words some of her pent
up anger toward him.

"He may not give me the time of day, but I've got
a lot of respect for him. He's got a fine business head
on those shoulders. Pour me some coffee, will you,
dear? Yes, he's done a lot with that marina property
he inherited from his old man."

Molly did not want to show too much interest in Brett and fire up Leland's imagination, but she was so curious she had to ask, "Did you say you knew his father?"

Leland took the proffered cup of coffee and shook his head sadly. "Yes, poor man. After his wife died he didn't hole up and stay all alone as I did. He went out in search of fun and lively companions until his dying day."

"And like father, like son."

"I know it's tempting to paint the father and son with the same brush. I've been guilty of it, myself. But it must have been hard on the boy. He could see what all the rest of us saw, I'm sure. That his father never did find the happiness he ran after so hard. If I'd been Brett, and grown up with that kind of example in front of me, I'd have found something different for my own life."

"But that's you. Brett is different. He seems to seek the same lifestyle that ruined his father; he craves the same sybaritic life."

"Oh, you college girls with your big words. You've got brains, Molly, I'll give you that. But look to your heart. Keep it fair and open. You never go wrong by trusting people and thinking the best of them."

If only Leland knew just how open her heart had been to Brett. And all she'd done was leave herself unprotected for the countless hurts he had inflicted upon her. This was one time she was going to discount Leland's advice. From now on her heart would be carefully shut away from Brett Sterling's reach.

"Is this dinner party tonight really necessary?" she asked as she took a cup of coffee back to her desk.

"Your mother's never seen my home; I've dragged

her to every restaurant in town. Now I want to show her some real hospitality."

Molly looked at Leland fondly, knowing how disappointed he would be if he should have to cancel any one of the entertainments he had planned for Charlotte. Taking a deep breath of resignation, she decided she would have to go through with what he'd planned for the evening. For the sake of the older couple, she would hide her discomfort and try to put on a happy enough face to fool them all.

"All right. You get Mrs. Okimoto to make her famous rum pie for dessert and I'll be there," she said.

"I'll go right now and give her that special request," he said, springing to his feet. She felt rewarded already by the sight of his happiness.

Molly had never seen her mother make such careful advance preparations for an evening. While Molly was still dawdling over her decisions about what to wear her mother applied her make up, and when Molly got out of the shower her mother was dressed and sitting with evening bag in hand on the white sofa.

"We don't have to be there until eight," Molly laughed. "And we don't want to arrive right on time."

"We most certainly do. Leland will be out on that front porch watching for us at one minute after. Now come on and get dressed, it's after seven already."

Molly picked out a pure silk shirtdress in a light lavender shade and went to set up an ironing board.

"Did you have to pick out something that needs pressing?" her mother sighed. "Here, let me do that for you."

Molly's plan was to arrive as late as possible, so

that she would minimize the time she had to spend in the presence of the dinner partner who had been picked out for her. Her mother, however, was hurrying her along and hovering over her so that they were in the car and on the way right on time. And just as her mother predicted, Leland greeted them as if they were an hour late. He ushered them proudly into the baronial living room of his home.

"Now Charlotte, you sit down right there on one of those love seats by the fireplace. I'll take you on a grand tour a little later, but right now let me fix you a drink."

"A little white wine will be fine," Charlotte said.

"I'll have the same," Molly told him, and she wandered the room restlessly, looking at the silver-framed photographs that crowded every tabletop just as if she'd never seen them before.

"Here's a picture of the boat Leland used to have," Molly said, taking one particular picture over to her mother.

Just then the doorbell sounded and Molly stiffened as if she'd been shot.

"That must be our young friend," Leland said. "Mrs. Okimoto's busy in the kitchen. I'll get the door if you'll finish this," he told Molly, indicating the filled wine glasses.

Molly took a glass to her mother determined to concentrate on what she was doing and not let her nervousness show. Her mother took the glass and then reached out to hold her daughter's cold hand in her own for a moment as both women listened to the sounds of conversation in the entry hall. Molly knew she would have to be very clever to fool her mother about her feelings toward Brett. She went over to the brass teacart that Leland had set up as a bar and reached out for her glass just as she heard the men enter the room.

Leland made the introductions. "Charlotte, I'd like you to meet Brett Sterling. Brett, this is Molly's mother, Charlotte Weston."

"How do you do, Mrs. Weston."

"And you know Molly, of course."

"Yes, I'm afraid after our long sail to Catalina Miss Weston knows me better than she cares to," Brett said, and his words were treated as sociable banter by Charlotte and Leland who chuckled with him good-naturedly.

As Leland brought Brett to the teacart to prepare him a drink, Molly moved away to sit on the love seat that faced the one her mother was sitting on. She was intrigued to see how comfortably Brett could fit into a drawing-room setting. This was the first time she had seen him dressed in a business suit, and all the untamed outdoor vitality of his tall frame seemed converted into pure elegance by the expert cut of the expensive dark blue mohair blend. His hair had been closely cropped, so that the curls she'd grown so used to were now stopped a bare inch into their swirl. She wondered if he'd had a haircut just for this evening, or because he was about to leave on a trip.

As Brett and Leland made small talk over the clinking of the ice bucket, Molly observed how carefully Brett had retracted his claws. He was still not warmly effusive with Leland, but his politeness could not be faulted as he inquired into the state of Leland's health and his feelings on the current business climate.

As Leland indicated to Brett with an extended arm that they join the ladies on the couches, Molly noticed that Brett walked straight toward her mother and sat beside her. And she didn't miss the heavy-lidded look of disdain in Brett's eyes as he watched Leland sit down beside Molly and pat her knee with happiness at how well the evening was going. She was glad the others would not recognize Brett's intent in pairing them off this way in the seating arrangement.

But Brett never missed a beat in his conversation with her mother. He was on his best behavior tonight, and not likely to reveal his contemptuous feelings about what he thought was going on between Molly and Leland. Apparently he assumed he was here as Charlotte's partner, and he intended to fulfill that obligation in a gentlemanly manner. Molly could feel some of her taut nerves begin to ease their hold on her, relieved that there would be no fireworks between them tonight.

Brett asked Charlotte about her hometown, and to Molly's surprise he told her he had once visited there when he was in the Navy, and he described how he loved the Cape Cod area. That was a subject that brought great delight to Charlotte, and they chatted amiably about it until the subject was exhausted. At last Brett leaned back and spoke to the couple across from him.

"I'm sorry, Mr. Gunther, that I will have to cut this evening short. I won't be able to accept your invitation to stay to dinner."

"I'm sorry to hear that."

"I'm leaving very early in the morning to take a cruise down to Baja and I guess you know all the preparation that entails. There's a lot we have to do tonight to get ready."

Molly knew from his use of the word "we" that Rita was going to be his traveling companion. No doubt the champagne had been consumed in celebration of her not very surprising decision to join him.

"We're very glad you could join us for a drink," Leland said. "It makes it more of a party to extend the group beyond the immediate family. If I may call myself a part of this family."

To Leland's merry smile, Molly had to respond. "Of course, Leland, after all you've done for us. It was the nicest surprise of my life when I found you'd brought mother out for a visit."

"And Molly does appreciate your surprises, doesn't she, Mr. Gunther?"

Leland seemed oblivious to any hidden meanings in Brett's words, but Molly noticed her mother's warm brown eyes express interest as she watched Brett send a brooding glance in Molly's direction.

There was a short pause in the conversation while all the participants took time to reconnoiter, and then Brett rose to his feet.

"My apologies, Mrs. Weston, for leaving without escorting you to dinner. I hope you have a good trip home. I'm sure it has been very reassuring for you to see your daughter so well established in her new life out here. Thank you for the drink, Mr. Gunther."

"Call me Leland, young man. Everyone else does."

"I've noticed that," Brett said. "Thank you."

Leland stood up, then reached down to take Molly's hand and pull her to her feet.

"Molly dear, will you take our guest to the door? I promised your mother I'd show her around the house, and before we sit down to eat would be a good time."

Molly let go of Leland's steadying hand reluctantly, and then had to hurry to follow Brett's strides to catch up with him before he disappeared into the entry hall. Just as they both reached the front door, Leland came hurrying up behind them.

He asked Brett, "About that boat charter we discussed on the phone yesterday. If you're going to be out of town—"

"I've told my assistant, Mr. McKenzie, all about it. Just talk to Mac and he'll arrange everything for you."

"That's fine. Thank you, Brett. And have a safe trip. Now Charlotte, come this way and I'll show you the office first."

Molly and Brett were alone in the entry hall, which was lit with only the candlelike bulbs of a chandelier suspended high above them in the stairwell. Brett's tanned face took on a dusky look, with the uneven lighting casting shadows from his long eyelashes across the sharp planes of his face.

"Now that your chaperone has left us, may I tell you how beautiful you look tonight?" he said.

"Thank you."

"Quite different from the way you looked when you left me on the dock last night."

"I should hope so," she tried to smile, but she was too suspicious of what he might say next to enjoy his compliments.

"You look just right sitting beside your Mr. Gunther in his living room, dressed in silk and wearing pearls. This is the proper setting for you, I can see that."

"I always enjoy visiting here."

"That's really the only reason I came here tonight. To tell you that I hope you'll be happy."

"And I hope you enjoy your cruise."

She drew back from him slightly, hoping to avoid one of those soul-shattering farewell kisses he so delighted in tormenting her with. This was, at last, their final good-bye, for by the time he returned her mother would be back home and Molly would be living again in the guest house, far from the marina and any further encounters with him. She struggled to keep her emotions in check, wanting to be adult during her last moments with him, and knowing that if he kissed her, he would shatter that tenuous hold she had on herself. But instead he reached up to touch her face, and he didn't seem to notice her shrink slightly from beneath his fingertips. His touch was more amorous to Molly than any kiss could have been.

"I still remember you the way you looked in Catalina. With your face all dark with sunburn, and those gold earrings on, you looked like a gypsy."

He was doubtless thinking about the cool white skin that would soon be beneath his touch on board the *Pleasure Seeker*. Rita was waiting for him right now, eager to help him forget his obsession with Molly, happy to put to rest his disappointment at never having conquered the one girl who resisted him.

He stepped back from her and reached behind him to open the huge oak door that swung open on squeaky hinges.

"Good-bye," he said, and then he disappeared into the night.

She leaned back against the door as if to bar it to his reentry. With a tired sigh she tried to close him out of her thoughts as well, but she was overcome with misgivings as she considered what might have been. If only her own expectations weren't so high. And if only he had been a different sort of man. If only . . .

But Brett operated under a double standard. He saw the rules for women as quite different from those for men. It was all right for him to keep Rita in his penthouse and aboard his boat, but he hated Molly for her supposed entanglement with Leland Gunther. If he had been less judgmental, less condemning, if they had been able to . . .

"There you are, little Molly. Now don't look so disappointed. We can still have a nice party with only three. Besides, when we get to the table I can guarantee you will cheer up." Leland's thin arms and scarecrow legs moved all at once and in four different directions as he led Charlotte and Molly into the dining room, obviously so buoyed up by the events of this evening that he didn't notice Molly's diffidence, and Charlotte's worried glances toward her.

The table was set with a fortune in antique silver. Two candelabras sat at each end flanking a large silver urn that held her mother's favorite white roses. But it was the silver champagne bucket standing next to Leland's place that he particularly called her attention to as he seated her across from her mother.

"There's a very important reason for this dinner, Molly. Your mother and I want to ask for your blessing, and if you give it, we'll break out this champagne and have some toasts." He sat down in his chair, his face suddenly serious. "I've asked Charlotte to marry me, and she has said she will."

"My blessing? Of course I give you my blessing. It's the most wonderful thing that could possibly happen. That two people I love so much could love each other. Why, it's perfect." She got up from her chair to go to her mother and kiss her on the cheek, then she went to Leland and did the same.

"We weren't sure you'd approve. It means giving up our home in the East," her mother said.

"But we'll all be together out here, and that's what matters. Oh, I was so afraid you two would never think of this. And I didn't want to push you."

"Oh, so now it was all your idea," Leland laughed, opening the champagne and filling their glasses.

Molly looked across at her mother, and her own

unhappiness melted away as she got caught up in the infectious high humor her mother radiated.

"Wait until you hear about the wedding we've planned! That's why we wanted Brett here, so we could make the rest of our plans after we'd announced our news," her mother said.

"That's all right. I told him what I want," Leland chuckled, proud of himself for working so quickly to bring his dream to life. "When I called him yesterday, I told him that I wanted to charter the biggest cruiser he could find for us. I told him I was planning a shipboard wedding in a couple of weeks and I wanted it to be very special. He said he'd start looking, and now he tells me he's put his best man in charge."

"Did you tell him who was getting married?" Molly asked through a tightly constricted throat.

"I was saving the official announcement for tonight," he said. "But I'm sure he could guess I was planning my own wedding party."

Molly put her hand to her face in an effort to restrain her shock. She was sure, too, that Brett had made a guess. And she was almost certain that he'd come up with the wrong guess. With Leland gushing to him on the phone, making little sense in his excitement, Brett must have assumed that the couple to be married would be Molly and Leland. He had wished her mother a safe journey home, so obviously he never thought for a moment that Charlotte was remaining here to be married.

"Brett probably thinks you're marrying me," Molly exclaimed, sharing her sorrow with them in spite of her vow to keep it to herself.

"Oh, no, Molly! Why would he think that?" Leland asked.

Charlotte Weston looked up from the salad plate

Mrs. Okimoto had just placed in front of her. "I can't imagine he'd believe such a thing," she said. "Doesn't he know that you're in love with him."

"Mother! What made you say that?"

"That was the only explanation I could think of for why you've been so upset lately."

"Well, put the thought out of your mind because he doesn't love me," she said, looking at Brett's empty chair at the end of the table as if he were sitting in it.

"Oh, Molly darling. Here we are so happy, planning our wedding—" her mother began.

"And I'm happy for you. We have lots to do, and lots of plans to make. So let's concentrate on that," Molly said, trying to close the subject.

Leland and Charlotte exchanged a worried look across the table, apparently unconvinced that Molly was taking the situation as lightly as she pretended. But since she rebuffed any further efforts from them to give sympathy or make suggestions, the subject was dropped and the rest of the evening was spent in discussing the happy future in store for Mr. and Mrs. Leland Gunther.

The next morning Molly sat on the balcony of her apartment. It was early, and her eyes felt heavy from a lack of sleep. Her night had been restless, with troubling thoughts hovering just out of reach of her conscious examination. Finally, just after dawn she had gotten up and fixed herself a cup of coffee so that she could sit and consider the possibilities that were disturbing her.

In spite of her determination to forget Brett Sterling, it was his actions during the past two days that she was now trying to reconstruct. She wanted to think logically and be methodical, putting everything into a firm timetable so that she would understand what had happened.

Let's see now. When Leland called Brett and invited him to dinner, he told him he wanted to charter a boat for a wedding. But he didn't say who was getting married. Brett accepted the dinner invitation, never mentioning anything at that time about leaving on a trip. So he must have decided that later. Was he upset when he began to suspect that I was marrying Leland? So upset that he planned to get away to put it out of his mind?

She stood up and let her thoughts move her agitatedly across the balcony.

Then he invited Rita for a sail so they could be alone to talk, and he took along a picnic to celebrate. Obviously, he planned to ask her to join him on his cruise. But then he ran into me by accident.

She went inside and refilled her cup, but put it down on the sink, forgetting to take it with her back outside.

In his stateroom on the boat, when he kissed me, when I almost . . . why, he thought I was already pledged to marry someone else. Did he think that I would change my mind? Did he think that a passionate love scene with him would save me from this disastrous mistake?

She remembered that he had accepted her rebuff more stoically than usual. Perhaps, just perhaps, she dared consider, he felt he had tried everything he could to save her, and by last night when she saw him at the dinner party, all he had left to do was offer her his rather unenthusiastic wish for happiness. She had to admit it was possible that all his actions might have been motivated by real caring.

If only Leland had told him on the phone, or the announcement had been made over cocktails before he left Leland's house, if only he'd learned that it was her mother that Leland loved, perhaps he would not have planned the trip, or invited Rita along. Maybe he would finally have seen that it was only his imagination, his suspicious nature, that had blinded him to the truth. He would realize that she was worthy of his affection, that she was not the type of girl to use and discard, but someone he could trust and even love.

Her excited musings had led her inside again and she was standing by the telephone before she realized what she planned to do.

I have to stop him. I have to let him know before he leaves with Rita.

She fumbled for the directory, and found the number for Sterling Enterprises. The phone rang and rang, and she looked at her watch, realizing it was only six o'clock in the morning. He said he liked to be out of the breakwater by eight o'clock. He might be getting dressed right this minute.

"Hello." It was Chuck's sleepy voice on the other end of the line.

"Chuck, this is Molly Weston. Is Brett there?"

"Didn't you know?" Chuck asked. "He left this morning for one of those get-away-from-it-all trips of his. They went down to the dock real early to get everything ready. Brett said he wanted to shove off before sunrise, I'm afraid he's far out to sea by this time. Molly? Are you there?"

"Yes, I heard you."

"I didn't go along for the send-off because Brett's making me finish that vacation that got washed out in Catalina. I'm leaving later today."

"Have a good time. And thank you, Chuck. It was nothing important. Just—just something about a charter."

"Oh, yeah, I remember. He said you'd be calling to arrange some party. He told Mac to take care of it. He should be back from the dock pretty soon and I'll have him call you. Brett wouldn't tell me anything about it. I guess he's still kind of mad at Mr. Gunther for dropping that boat deal. He didn't want to talk about it."

"Yes, I know he's mad at Mr. Gunther. Goodbye, Chuck."

Molly's work at the office kept her mercifully busy during the next two weeks. Mac proved to be surprisingly well organized and called almost every day, describing the 125-foot cruise ship he'd found for them to use, and coordinating the flowers and food that would have to be taken aboard for the ceremony day.

Charlotte was often at Leland's home with Molly now. She was learning the routine of the household and making long distance telephone calls to invite out-of-town people to the wedding. Leland and Charlotte seemed to have endless outings planned that always required Molly's presence. She was occupied with luncheons and shopping trips and interviews with caterers and musicians.

Molly and her mother were returning from a busy morning of errands when they entered their apartment to hear the phone ringing. Molly's arms were laden with packages, and Charlotte was carefully juggling the two dressbags they'd just brought from the dressmaker containing her own beige chiffon wedding dress and a filmy cream-colored chiffon that had been made for Molly to wear. Charlotte took the call and Molly assumed she was talking to Mac for there seemed to be some last-minute wedding details to be worked out.

When she got off the phone, Charlotte said, "Apparently the boat owner wants his deposit. I told her you'll bring a check up right away."

"I thought that was Mac," Molly said, sinking onto the couch, tired after the hectic morning.

"No, it was that girl who works for Brett. Rita? Is that her name?"

"Is that who you were talking to?"

"Yes, I guess she's helping Mac with the arrangements."

Molly stood up, alert to the news. So, Rita and Brett had returned already from their idyllic cruise.

Her mother was burrowing through her purse. "Fortunately Leland gave me the money just this morning. Now where did I put that check? Here it is, will you run it upstairs to the penthouse, dear? I'd better get busy unwrapping all this."

Molly took the check and left the apartment without stopping to comb her hair or freshen her makeup. If Brett was back then he had probably already heard from Mac the news that would come as such a shock to him. She was so anxious to see his reaction that she didn't care about her appearance, and she didn't want to waste a minute.

He must have been told by now the names of the happy wedding couple, there was no way that the confusion could continue with Mac so heavily involved in the wedding plans. And if he hadn't for some reason been told, she would tell him herself and watch for her moment of vindication. Now that he'd spent so much time with Rita, it was probably too late to ever break him away from her, but at least Molly would see respect on Brett's face for the very first time.

When Rita answered the door of the penthouse, Molly gaped at her with open amazement. The girl was certainly not dressed for any administrative duties. She was wearing a shimmery hostess caftan of a gauzy material so transparent that little of the lean beauty of her body was left to the imagination.

"Oh, Molly. I didn't mean you had to bring the money up right now. Mac just said we have to get it to the man before the wedding. That's still two days away."

"Am I interrupting something?" Molly said with a cold tone that she hoped would match the unwelcoming words with which the girl had greeted her.

"I'm trying to fix a very special dinner, and, oh dear—" Rita turned suddenly and hurried away, making a clicking sound with her spike-heeled gold sandals as they slapped on the parquet floor.

Molly stood for a moment with check in hand wondering what to do next, then hearing a crash and a bang from behind the door where Rita had disappeared, she hesitantly went to see what was wrong. The big kitchen was in a state of complete chaos. Rita was in the middle of the room helplessly waving her long slender arms in the cumbersome sleeves of her dress.

"I don't know what to do next. I'm not a very good cook, and I want everything to turn out just right."

"Why don't you start by putting on an apron over that gorgeous dress? And then roll up the sleeves so you don't set yourself on fire," Molly said, finding herself talking to Rita just as Brett always did, slowly and carefully as one might speak to a high-strung child.

Then Molly set to work helping the girl get organized. She placed a couple of dirty pans out of the way in the sink, clearing a work space. Rita had cut a recipe for lobster Newburg from the newspaper and the clipping was wet and wrinkled. As Molly fastened it neatly to the refrigerator door so the girl could refer to it, she glanced across the eating bar into the dining room.

The table overlooking the harbor view had been set for a romantic dinner for two. There was a single carnation in a bud vase, and candles stood ready for a match. Two plates, two sets of silver, two wine glasses, two water goblets sat on their two place mats like pairs of animals waiting to enter Noah's Ark. Indeed Molly had interrupted something, and now she was in a hurry to leave. Apparently Brett and Rita planned to be alone together to reminisce about the important journey they'd just completed.

"Give this check to Brett, will you?" Molly said, pointing to where she'd put it on the sink.

"Brett isn't here."

"Well, when he returns. And good luck with your dinner."

Rita's flurry of nerves seemed to have died down and she followed Molly back to the door.

"Thank you, Molly. I wish you could stay and help me cook it. Say, how have you been? I haven't seen you in awhile. You look a little down."

"Well, I can't say the same for you. You look radiant."

"These have been the happiest two weeks of my life. There's usually so many people around, and everyone so busy. Just to be quiet and alone, with time to talk with no interruptions, that's the way to really get to know a man. I think I've finally been able to see my life clearly and make the right plans for the future. That's why I want to make tonight extra-special."

Molly wondered just how much hurt she was capable of taking. Rita seemed to be putting her to that test, her every word stabbing at Molly as she made her way out of the apartment. With relief she heard the door slam behind her. Any last secret shred of hope she'd nurtured was now dead. Brett was lost forever to her for he had found love somewhere else.

In just two days the wedding would be over, her mother would be established in her new life, and Molly could pack up her things and return to Massachusetts. She'd get her mother to keep their old house and she'd go there and live in it. In time, amid familiar surroundings, alone, she might be able to heal herself from all that she had suffered. Her only chance of forgetting Brett Sterling was to put as much distance as possible between them.

Chapter Nine

Molly and her mother loaded their dresses carefully in the car and drove to the dock early on Saturday morning. The weather couldn't have been better for a wedding. Just being out in the bright sunshine and feeling the fragrance of the summer breezes in the air helped Molly to put her own sadness behind her and look toward the exciting promise of the day.

The ceremony was to be at noon, followed by a buffet luncheon. But when they arrived at the dock, dozens of workmen were already scurrying about, and Molly and Charlotte had to dodge between them to go on board and find the main stateroom where they could get dressed.

"I never expected anything like this! Why this looks like one of those big white cruise ships that tours the Greek islands," Charlotte said with a trace of nervousness.

"You've invited thirty-five people. We had to find

a yacht big enough to handle the crowd," Molly laughed. "Mac is resourceful. This ship was docked in the Sterling Marina. Some millionaire owns it and Mac convinced him he should charter it out for the day. Isn't it beautiful!"

"Yes, but when I think of all the people who are coming—is everything ready?"

"Of course, you know that. We've thought of everything. And what we've forgotten, Mac has taken care of. I've been quite surprised at what a romantic fellow he is. He's the one who suggested decorating the dock. Did you see the men bringing all those plants and baskets of flowers?"

Charlotte's face was pale as she sat in the cabin contemplating the elaborate wedding production in which she was soon to star. The life she would be leading as Mrs. Leland Gunther would be quite different from the quiet life she'd left behind her. Money would no longer be an impediment to any plan. Everything she did from now on would be elegant and luxurious. At the moment she was staggered by the thought of the complicated responsibilities that would also be hers.

"Molly, won't you change your mind about moving back home? When I come back from my honeymoon, I want to find you here. I'll need you to help me. Leland will need a new secretary, and I'll have that house to run. It will be awful without you."

"When you get back, I'll still be here. But as soon as we've hired someone to replace me, I'm going home. You know I have to get away."

"Yes, I know you want to. But I'm hoping you'll change your mind."

"You're just suffering prenuptial jitters, mother. Now stretch out here on this berth and rest. You have plenty of time before you have to dress. I'm going to get changed and then go out there and run down my checklist and make sure that everything's done."

Molly slipped the soft chiffon dress over her head, surprised at how feminine she felt as soon as the flounces and swirls had settled into place. The bodice of the dress was completely adrift with carefully gathered ruffles of the chiffon covering Molly's ample bosom, but at the same time dipping to reveal a provocative cleavage at the neckline. She'd never worn such an expensive custom-made dress, and she stood looking at the transformation in the mirror. She'd kept her hair simple; fresh and clean, it cascaded in a simple fall to her shoulders as she brushed its coppery length.

"Where are the flowers for your hair?" her mother said tensely.

"I'll put them on later. Now you just rest and I'll be back to help you in a little while."

Once she had her mother settled down she took her efficiently typed list of reminders and went out to see that everyone was doing what needed to be done.

She stood on the side deck of the boat and looked down at the dock. Mac was instructing the men who were unloading a truck that was parked dockside. They were bringing pots of blooming azaleas and placing them so that they formed a flowery walkway up to the gangplank. Two large topiary trees in the redwood containers stood at the bottom of the ramp, and Mac was wrapping white crepe paper around every inch of railing on the dock.

"That looks beautiful, Mac. You've done a wonderful job," she called. He looked up to see her, and then came up the gangplank toward her with his typically nimble seaman's stride, his hands never requiring a touch of the handrails.

"I'm in charge of decorating out here, and Rita's taken over inside. She'd have roses wound around the wheel if I hadn't stopped her. I told her I've skippered a lot of strange vessels in my day, but never a floating flower garden like this."

"Thank you for all you've done."

"This is more fun that I've ever had. The Sterling Anchorage has never looked so shipshape. It's a shame to stop at just one wedding. I told Rita we ought to go ahead and make it a doubleheader."

Molly blinked her eyes rapidly with the shock of Mac's words. Mac was Brett's closest friend, and as such he must have been made aware of how the relationship between Rita and Brett was deepening. If he could tease Rita about the subject, then he must know that marriage plans were in the wind.

She turned away from him to hide her enveloping emotions. "I think that one wedding today is all I could stand," she said in almost a whisper.

"After planning this one, the next one will be easy," he laughed heartily, and he skipped back down the gangplank to greet a group of musicians who had arrived and were unpacking their instruments just below.

Before going inside to check on the galley, Molly stood for a moment wiping her eyes where a tear had left a bitter sting. Then she stepped through a sliding door into the salon. It was a large room, with windows all the way around that let in the cloudless blue of the sky. Humming to herself in one corner of the room was Rita. She was dressed in a conservative blue skirt and white blouse to identify her as one of the crew, but she looked as gay as the mixed bouquet of flowers she was arranging with fluttery gestures.

"Thank you for coming to help today, Rita," Molly said.

"I just love weddings, don't you?" Rita said. "Does this look all right?" She backed away from her arrangement on the buffet table to study it critically. She didn't wait for Molly's answer, but darted back to adjust a long stem or two and continued. "Yes, everyone's here. When Sterling Enterprises takes on a project we bring out all the troops. Chuck got back yesterday, and he's down below counting out champagne glasses. I even think Brett is coming, too. I talked to him last night."

Molly had never considered the possibility that Brett might come with them. He had turned over all the planning to Mac, and Molly had assumed he was glad to be rid of any further contact with the Gunther wedding party.

"I told him your mother loved white roses and I hadn't been able to find any. Brett's the one who suggested we fly them in. He said the bride should have just what she wants. When I get married, I'm going to have gardenias. Bowls and bowls of them, everywhere. And I'm going to carry white orchids."

Molly turned away and headed for the galley, leaving Rita alone, still spinning out her exciting plans for the future, unaware that Molly could not bear to listen.

The cateress was busily at work preparing trays of cold meats and bowls of salad. Molly told her the final guest count, and was heading back toward the top deck when she almost bumped into Chuck Yancey who was carrying a tray of glasses.

"Hey, Molly, look out. You're not watching where you're going."

"I'm glad to see you, Chuck. I heard you just got back from your vacation. How was Catalina?"

"It was neat! But I'm glad to come back and get in on all this. Do you want to serve any champagne before the ceremony, or should I wait to bring these out afterward?"

"I think we'll wait. As soon as everyone's on board we'll cast off, then when Mac finds a good place to anchor, we'll have the ceremony. After that, the party begins."

"Mac and Rita seem to have everything under control," he said. "When I got home and offered my help, they treated me like an intruder. I don't think they cared one bit that I was back. They were very happy taking care of things all alone. Say, is that what I think I see?" Chuck leaned over to a nearby porthole, then grabbed Molly's hand and began to pull her toward a stairway.

"What is it? What do you see?"

"Right off our starboard side. It's Brett's boat. He did make it back!"

Chuck was pulling Molly out onto the forward deck before she could protest. And sure enough, coming alongside was the *Pleasure Seeker*.

"Where has he been?" Molly asked.

"He's been gone for two weeks, you knew that."

"But I thought he'd gotten back a few days ago from that trip. I saw Rita—"

"He called us by radiophone last night and he wasn't in any hurry to get home until Rita started babbling on and on about the wedding plans. He didn't even know who was getting married so he started asking her all kinds of questions. I guess he's changed his attitude toward Mr. Gunther, because all of a sudden he said he would sail all night to get home in time to go along with us."

"Then he's just getting back from Baja? He went all by himself?"

"Sure, I told you how he loves to do that. I guess he had some problems on his mind. But when I got on the phone with him, he sounded like his old self. Hey, hi there old buddy," Chuck called out as soon as Brett's boat was directly beside them.

Brett's boat seemed dwarfed by their larger vessel as he stood looking up at Molly and Chuck standing on the deck high above him. His clothing was rumpled and damp, his aquiline nose bright with sunburn, and his chin covered with a stubble of beard, but he had never looked so handsome to Molly before. His eyes, when they caught hers, held fast, and he stared into her face as if she were the safe harbor he had been sailing toward all night.

"How was the trip, Brett? Where are you going to dock, over at that next pier? Want me to come and tie you down?" Sometimes Chuck, just like his sister, was too impatient to wait for answers. He rushed away to be ready to help Brett.

"The sailor is home from the sea," Brett called to Molly, giving her an unblinking look she was too confused to try to interpret.

"I hear you're coming aboard to join us," she said.

Brett reached up and rubbed his jaw. "I'm not in the best shape for a party. But I wouldn't miss this one. Tell Mac not to shove off until I get there."

He pushed the throttle of the boat forward and for the first time since she'd caught sight of him, he looked away from her to steer his boat away. Molly leaned back against a cabin door behind her, trying to readjust her thinking to these startling new facts.

Rita had not gone along with Brett, so what was she talking about when she raved about the happiest two weeks of her life? And why was she planning the romantic dinner for two when Brett had gone off on his cruise and sent Chuck away on his vacation, leaving only Mac and Rita behind?

Molly crossed the foredeck and went to the port

side to stand looking down at the decorated dock. The trucks were gone, the workmen had disappeared, and Mac and Rita were standing alone admiring their handiwork. Mac went to adjust a paper garland, then Rita moved a pot of flowers a few inches to the left, then they stood smiling at each other, and Mac held his arms open toward the girl. The tiny blonde went to him with a happy laugh, and they stood together, their arms about each other's shoulders.

Molly felt a surge of happiness that weakened her knees as she gripped the handrail in front of her and let herself share their joy. Now she understood the decision that Rita had sought Brett's advice about before he left. Mac had offered her his love, and she'd been uncertain about taking it. But with Brett away on his odyssey, and Chuck sent off on vacation, Rita had obviously had time alone with Mac in which to learn to accept and appreciate what he wanted to give her.

Mac was a rock of a man, older and wise about the world. And Rita needed just this kind of firm loving guidance in her life. Mac could offer her exciting trips to faraway places, all the change and stimulation that she craved, but he could also offer her the security she needed. Mac has spoken this morning about another wedding, and the thought had ripped the last vestige of Molly's hopes. But now she knew what he had meant, and she could give her ardent blessing to the girl who wanted to carry white orchids and marry Mac.

Molly was disturbed from her reverie by the sight of the first few wedding guests slowly strolling down the dock admiring the decorations and chatting among themselves. She had to tell the mariachi band to begin playing on the dock, the minister had to be shown where to conduct the service, Leland wasn't here yet and there were guests to be greeted, and she'd promised to help her mother dress. She rushed to see to her responsibilities. She had no time now to think about her own life.

Later, as Molly was helping her mother pin her large picture hat into place, she felt a throb beneath her feet. She realized that Mac was starting the engines.

"Oh, Mother, I'll be right back. I've forgotten to tell Mac something. We can't leave the dock yet."

She hurried up to the wheelhouse and found Mac shouting orders through the window to his dock crew as they untied the lines and lifted the gangplank. The guests were all on board and lined up on the deck of the ship throwing colored paper streamers down toward the musicians who were playing spirited Mexican music to bid the ship farewell.

"Mac, don't cast off yet. Brett is coming. He told me to tell you to wait for him."

"Brett was just here. Now that he's signed on, my first mate tells me we have to get under way. Rita wants everything to go exactly according to the schedule I set up."

"I've never seen her work so hard to please someone. Sounds as though you've found the perfect first mate."

"Indeed I have."

"I never suspected you two were interested in each other, but now that I know about it, it seems very logical."

"I thought everyone could tell how I felt. She ran her flag up my mast the first time I ever saw her. Imagine, an old son of a sea cook like me."

"I'm happy for you." She leaned over and gave him a kiss on the cheek. "Congratulations."

Mac let out a lusty laugh. "Don't let Brett catch you passing out kisses."

"Why not?" Molly asked. Her voice was teasing and she knew it. But she wanted to find out what Mac thought about her relationship to the man who was like a son to him.

"I think I know why he was so anxious to come along on this wedding party. He wants to keep an eye on you, and I can't blame him a bit. He's a jealous sort, you can be sure of that."

"Do you think so?" she said, the happy tease still lighting her eyes. She knew better than anyone about Brett's jealousy. That was what had kept them apart. He had resented her every moment with Leland Gunther. Now all she needed was an opportunity to convince Brett Sterling that he had always been the only man for her.

Mac turned his attention to navigating the boat away from the dock, and Molly was brought back to the immediate present.

"I haven't seen Leland yet. Are you sure he's here?" Molly asked Mac.

"Do you think I'd pull out and leave the groom behind? He's here all right, and eager as a teenager to get this wedding started."

"I think I'll go find him and make sure he's not planning to jump ship before the ceremony."

"I don't think there's any chance of that," Mac laughed.

Leland was in the main salon, mingling with his guests and obviously enjoying himself immensely. He had planned to spend this time before the ceremony acting as host, while adhering to the old tradition and keeping the bride secreted away until she emerged for the ceremony.

"Molly, you look as beautiful as you should look on your own wedding day," he greeted her, taking her hand and stepping back to regard her with paternal pride. "If your mother looks as good in her new duds, we're going to have one wingding of a wedding."

"You look pretty dapper yourself," Molly said, adjusting the boutonniere on the lapel of his dark suit.

"Say, I just saw Brett Sterling and he's a changed man. He fell all over himself telling me what a wise choice I've made and offering me good wishes."

"You just spoke to him?"

"I tried to explain to him why I won't be doing any more boat shopping for awhile. I told him I've found a woman to love and that's more than enough to satisfy me. You know what he said?"

"No, what?" she said absently, looking around to see where Brett had disappeared.

"He said what he wants for himself is to have both. A woman to love and a boat to carry them wherever they want to go together. Now what do you suppose that young man has in mind?" Leland's eyes sparkled with understanding.

Molly remembered her envy as she'd pictured Brett and Rita enjoying the *Pleasure Seeker* together. All she wanted in life was to be the one to travel with Brett, live with him, share both his adventurous moods and his periods of contentment. She could only pray that he had come to the same decision.

Leland turned away to answer a question from one of the guests, and Molly realized she must return to be with her mother. As she made her way back to the cabin, she kept her head moving in all directions, certain that she would spot Brett somewhere.

"Molly, you just missed Brett," her mother said as soon as she'd opened the door. Molly let out a disgusted sigh, wondering how it was possible that she was always ten steps behind him when they were both confined to the area of this boat, and when she was trembling with the anticipation of wanting to talk with him.

Her mother was fastening a silver chain around her neck. "I was fussing because I'd forgotten I needed something 'borrowed' to wear today, so he loaned me this."

Molly reached over to examine the pendant that now dangled at her mother's throat.

Charlotte explained, "It's a St. Christopher's medal that he always wears. He told me it was given to him by his mother."

Molly turned the medal over and began to laugh, the joke on her lips prompting her to spill out the abundance of happiness that was overfilling her heart. "Look, Mother. It even has his name engraved on it. See, Sterling."

Her mother laughed with her, taking her daughter into her arms. "That's because it's silver. I'm not so distracted today that I'd fall for that. Now sit down a minute. I want to tell you what Brett and I talked about."

Molly fell back onto a chair, anxious to hear every word.

"I was telling Brett how hard it was for me when I had to send you out here to California," Charlotte began. "I told him that I was only able to do it because I trusted Leland to look after you and protect you, and it was that trust in him that led me to love him. But he understood how hard it was for me to let you go. He told me he has had the same problem with two young people who've been in his care. He's had to force himself to let them go out on their own, and he's been rewarded to see what good decisions they've made, how strong they've become."

Molly realized that Brett had been talking about

Rita and Chuck, and that he must totally agree with Rita's decision to marry Mac. How could she have let herself suspect his relationship with Rita when it was as protective and innocent as Leland's concern for her?

Charlotte went on, "Molly, he's a very loving, caring man. I just hope that it's not too late for you two. I hope that the differences you've had with him in the past can be forgotten."

"I hope so, too," Molly said quietly.

Her mother turned to the mirror to begin her final inspection. She was so preoccupied now with her own thoughts that Molly didn't want to break her mood with any more conversation. When they both felt the boat slow to a stop, and the engines cut off, they knew the ceremony was only a few minutes away. There was a knock at the door. Rita came in with a large white box.

"Here are your flowers. This bouquet is for you, Mrs. Weston. And Molly, here's yours, and here's the wreath for your hair. I'll stand outside the door here and watch for Chuck's wave. When he puts on the record of the wedding march, he'll let us know."

From outside the cabin Molly heard the sound of the familiar wedding music. She gave her mother's shoulders a final embrace of reassurance, and stepped outside to wait beside Rita for her cue. They both saw Chuck's wave, and Molly started to walk forward to the bow of the ship.

The guests were standing on the broad foredeck in the sunshine. At the prow of the ship the minister stood between two baskets of white flowers. Leland stood close by. At the right of Leland she saw Brett, watching her approach with a curiously blank expression on his face.

Molly gripped her bouquet more tightly, and tried to give Brett a tremulous smile, but he didn't return it. He stood with his lips slightly parted, his eyes unreadable, as he watched her walk toward him.

"Dearly beloved, we are gathered together here in the sight of God, and in the face of this company, to join this man and this woman in holy matrimony."

Molly's eyelids fluttered in an attempt to keep the threatening tears from materializing in her eyes. It was impossible to look anywhere but into Brett's face, for he was standing directly in front of her now, facing her before the minister's solemn liturgy as surely as if the words were directed at the two of them.

"Wilt thou love her, comfort her, honor and keep her . . ."

Molly looked down for just a moment at the flowers shaking in her hands. Was it too late? Could she and Brett ever forget the bitter words they had exchanged? Could the misunderstanding which had kept them apart ever be put to rest?

Leland's rasping voice had new dignity as he repeated his vow. "To have and to hold, from this day forward, for better or worse . . ."

If only Brett would give her some sign, some indication of how he felt as he listened to the unbreakable vows being repeated. But he only watched her with eyes that seemed to reflect the entire arc of blue sky that surrounded them.

Charlotte's voice was soft. "With this ring I thee wed . . ."

Molly caught a flicker of movement from the corner of her eye and then noticed that Rita and Mac had moved up to the edge of the crowd to join the spectators. Mac was holding her hand tightly. Their expressions were rapt as they seemed to be rehearsing for the sacrament they would soon share.

"I pronounce that they are husband and wife. Let us pray."

At last Brett's unwavering gaze left her, and Molly bowed her head, adding her own private supplications to those being offered in the name of the newly married pair. And then suddenly the ritual was over. Leland was trying to duck his head beneath Charlotte's huge hat to give her the kiss that would seal his commitment. Soon there was a flood of conversation as everyone began wishing the pair well and moving about to get close to them.

"Throw that bouquet, Mrs. Gunther," Leland instructed his new wife. "You can't shake hands and kiss everyone with that bunch of flowers in the way."

Molly was unprepared, shaken so abruptly from her private thoughts. She saw her mother suddenly throw the white roses into the air. She saw everyone move back out of the way, and then she realized that Mac had given Rita a little push. The girl jumped forward to stand in the center of the grouping directly under the bouquet, catching it easily. There was applause and a murmur of delighted approval.

"Just a minute," Brett called out, and everyone stopped talking to turn and look at him. He went to Rita and took the flowers from her hand. "I don't think that was a fair catch."

"Oh, Brett," Rita cajoled. "You know what this means. Now I will be the next bride."

"We'll just see about that," he said, as Molly moved out from behind the crowd to watch him.

Brett's strong hands were pulling the flowers apart, ripping them from the fastenings that held them in a formal arrangement. The onlookers seemed stunned by his actions. Charlotte gave her daughter a worried look, obviously wondering what Brett was doing. He had certainly attracted everyone's attention.

Leland, aware of Brett's volatile nature, seemed afraid an unpleasant scene would mar the perfection of this day. He stepped forward as if to take the flowers away from Brett.

"Now see here young man. Let's not spoil the tradition—"

"Who's spoiling a tradition? I merely want to spread some of this good luck around."

As though in a dream, Molly stepped forward, the significance of Brett's gestures dawning on her. He had formed the flowers into two distinct bundles, and he handed one back to Rita, who was pouting prettily beside him.

"Where is it written that two bridal bouquets cannot be caught?" He took the remaining white roses, wrapped them quickly with a dangling piece of florist's tape and then looked up at Molly.

She was not caught unawares this time. She put her own flowers down on a nearby hatch cover and then stood ready, facing him. He lobbed the flowers across to her with an easy throw, and Molly caught them and clasped them tightly against her bosom.

"Two more brides! Two more weddings. Oh, how exciting," came an outburst from Rita. Mac put a firm arm around her shoulder and led her away, reminding her that they still had duties to perform. After cheering Brett's sentimental move, the crowd started moving off the foredeck and toward the salon where the party would now begin.

Leland and Charlotte stopped for just a moment to give Molly their whispered congratulations before going to join the others. They knew how much more they had to celebrate now that Molly's future was as assured as theirs.

"Molly, will you marry me?"

She was not sure she could believe that she was finally hearing the words she'd so much wanted to hear Brett say. She looked around, realizing that they were the only ones left on the deck. They seemed to be alone in the world as they drifted out in the ocean, surrounded by miles of water on all sides.

"Yes, I will." She crossed to him carefully, aware that, just as on that first day she had met him, she was again wearing shoes inappropriate for where she was stepping. She slipped into his arms.

"On one condition. I want a silver wedding band that says Sterling on the inside."

Brett laughed. "You don't want diamonds? Won't you let me spend my money on you?"

"No, thank you. All I want is you." She reached up to stroke his freshly shaven cheek.

"Oh, I know. All you're ever going to ask me for is lots of books to read and the biggest boat I can afford."

"Any boat will do."

"How about the *Princess?* We need a boat that the two of us can manage alone when we want to get away from it all. But we'll need lots of cabin space for the children someday."

"But will you sell the *Pleasure Seeker?*"

"My love, I don't need the *Pleasure Seeker* anymore. I have the pleasure that my heart was seeking, right here in my arms."

IT'S YOUR OWN SPECIAL TIME

Contemporary romances for today's women.
Each month, six very special love stories will be yours
from SILHOUETTE. Look for them wherever books are sold
or order now from the coupon below.

$1.50 each

- ___# 1 PAYMENT IN FULL Hampson
- ___# 2 SHADOW AND SUN Carroll
- ___# 3 AFFAIRS OF THE HEART Powers
- ___# 4 STORMY MASQUERADE Hampson
- ___# 5 PATH OF DESIRE Goforth
- ___# 6 GOLDEN TIDE Stanford
- ___# 7 MIDSUMMER BRIDE Lewis
- ___# 8 CAPTIVE HEART Beckman
- ___# 9 WHERE MOUNTAINS WAIT Wilson
- ___#10 BRIDGE OF LOVE Caine
- ___#11 AWAKEN THE HEART Vernon
- ___#12 UNREASONABLE SUMMER Browning
- ___#13 PLAYING FOR KEEPS Hastings
- ___#14 RED, RED ROSE Oliver
- ___#15 SEA GYPSY Michaels
- ___#16 SECOND TOMORROW Hampson
- ___#17 TORMENTING FLAME John
- ___#18 THE LION'S SHADOW Hunter
- ___#19 THE HEART NEVER FORGETS Thornton
- ___#20 ISLAND DESTINY Fulford
- ___#21 SPRING FIRES Richards
- ___#22 MEXICAN NIGHTS Stephens
- ___#23 BEWITCHING GRACE Edwards
- ___#24 SUMMER STORM Healy
- ___#25 SHADOW OF LOVE Stanford
- ___#26 INNOCENT FIRE Hastings
- ___#27 THE DAWN STEALS SOFTLY Hampson
- ___#28 MAN OF THE OUTBACK Hampson
- ___#29 RAIN LADY Wildman
- ___#30 RETURN ENGAGEMENT Dixon
- ___#31 TEMPORARY BRIDE Halldorson
- ___#32 GOLDEN LASSO Michaels
- ___#33 A DIFFERENT DREAM Vitek
- ___#34 THE SPANISH HOUSE John
- ___#35 STORM'S END Stanford
- ___#36 BRIDAL TRAP McKay
- ___#37 THE BEACHCOMBER Beckman
- ___#38 TUMBLED WALL Browning
- ___#39 PARADISE ISLAND Sinclair
- ___#40 WHERE EAGLES NEST Hampson
- ___#41 THE SANDS OF TIME Owen
- ___#42 DESIGN FOR LOVE Powers
- ___#43 SURRENDER IN PARADISE Robb
- ___#44 DESERT FIRE Hastings
- ___#45 TOO SWIFT THE MORNING Carroll
- ___#46 NO TRESPASSING Stanford
- ___#47 SHOWERS OF SUNLIGHT Vitek
- ___#48 A RACE FOR LOVE Wildman
- ___#49 DANCER IN THE SHADOWS Wisdom
- ___#50 DUSKY ROSE Scott
- ___#51 BRIDE OF THE SUN Hunter
- ___#52 MAN WITHOUT A HEART Hampson
- ___#53 CHANCE TOMORROW Browning
- ___#54 LOUISIANA LADY Beckman
- ___#55 WINTER'S HEART Ladame
- ___#56 RISING STAR Trent
- ___#57 TO TRUST TOMORROW John
- ___#58 LONG WINTER'S NIGHT Stanford
- ___#59 KISSED BY MOONLIGHT Vernon
- ___#60 GREEN PARADISE Hill

__ #61 WHISPER MY NAME Michaels	__ #80 WONDER AND WILD DESIRE Stephens
__ #62 STAND-IN BRIDE Halston	__ #81 IRISH THOROUGHBRED Roberts
__ #63 SNOWFLAKES IN THE SUN Brent	__ #82 THE HOSTAGE BRIDE Dailey
__ #64 SHADOW OF APOLLO Hampson	__ #83 LOVE LEGACY Halston
__ #65 A TOUCH OF MAGIC Hunter	__ #84 VEIL OF GOLD Vitek
__ #66 PROMISES FROM THE PAST Vitek	__ #85 OUTBACK SUMMER John
__ #67 ISLAND CONQUEST Hastings	__ #86 THE MOTH AND THE FLAME Adams
__ #68 THE MARRIAGE BARGAIN Scott	__ #87 BEYOND TOMORROW Michaels
__ #69 WEST OF THE MOON St. George	__ #88 AND THEN CAME DAWN Stanford
__ #70 MADE FOR EACH OTHER Afton Bonds	__ #89 A PASSIONATE BUSINESS James
__ #71 A SECOND CHANCE ON LOVE Ripy	__ #90 WILD LADY Major
__ #72 ANGRY LOVER Beckman	__ #91 WRITTEN IN THE STARS Hunter
__ #73 WREN OF PARADISE Browning	__ #92 DESERT DEVIL McKay
__ #74 WINTER DREAMS Trent	__ #93 EAST OF TODAY Browning
__ #75 DIVIDE THE WIND Carroll	__ #94 ENCHANTMENT Hampson
__ #76 BURNING MEMORIES Hardy	__ #95 FOURTEEN KARAT BEAUTY Wisdom
__ #77 SECRET MARRIAGE Cork	__ #96 LOVE'S TREACHEROUS JOURNEY Beckman
__ #78 DOUBLE OR NOTHING Oliver	__ #97 WANDERER'S DREAM Clay
__ #79 TO START AGAIN Halldorson	__ #98 MIDNIGHT WINE St. George
	__ #99 TO HAVE, TO HOLD Camp

$1.75 each

__ # 100 YESTERDAY'S SHADOW Stanford	__ # 106 THE LANCASTER MEN Dailey
__ # 101 PLAYING WITH FIRE Hardy	__ # 107 TEARS OF MORNING Bright
__ # 102 WINNER TAKE ALL Hastings	__ # 108 FASCINATION Hampson
__ # 103 BY HONOUR BOUND Cork	__ # 112 WHISPER WIND Stanford
__ # 104 WHERE THE HEART IS Vitek	__ # 113 WINTER BLOSSOM Browning
__ # 105 MISTAKEN IDENTITY Eden	__ # 114 PAINT ME RAINBOWS Michaels
__ # 109 FIRE UNDER SNOW Vernon	__ # 115 A MAN FOR ALWAYS John
__ # 110 A STRANGER'S WIFE Trent	__ # 116 AGAINST THE WIND Lindley
__ # 111 WAYWARD LOVER South	__ # 117 MANHATTAN MASQUERADE Scott

- - - - - - - - - - - - - - - - - - - -

SILHOUETTE BOOKS. Department SB/1

1230 Avenue of the Americas
New York, NY 10020

Please send me the books I have checked above. I am enclosing
$_____ (please add 50¢ to cover postage and handling. NYS and
NYC residents please add appropriate sales tax). Send check or
money order—no cash or C.O.D.'s please. Allow six weeks for delivery.

NAME_____

ADDRESS_____

CITY_____STATE/ZIP_____

Introducing
First Love from
Silhouette *Romances for teenage girls to build their dreams on.*

They're wholesome, fulfilling, supportive novels about every young girl's dreams. Filled with the challenges, excitement— and responsibilities—of love's first blush, *First Love* paperbacks prepare young adults to stand at the threshold of maturity with confidence and composure.

Introduce your daughter, or some young friend to the *First Love* series by giving her a one-year subscription to these romantic originals, written by leading authors. She'll receive two NEW $1.75 romances each month, a total of 24 books a year. Send in your coupon now. **There's nothing quite as special as a First Love.**

15-Day Free Trial Offer
6 Silhouette Romances

6 Silhouette Romances, free for 15 days! We'll send you 6 new Silhouette Romances to keep for 15 days, absolutely free! If you decide not to keep them, send them back to us. You pay nothing.

Free Home Delivery. But if you enjoy them as much as we think you will, keep them by paying the invoice enclosed with your free trial shipment. We'll pay all shipping and handling charges. You get the convenience of Home Delivery and we pay the postage and handling charge each month.

Don't miss a copy. The Silhouette Book Club is the way to make sure you'll be able to receive every new romance we publish before they're sold out. There is no minimum number of books to buy and you can cancel at any time.

This offer expires April 30, 1982

Silhouette Book Club, Dept. **SBI**17B
120 Brighton Road, Clifton, NJ 07012

Please send me 6 Silhouette Romances to keep for 15 days, absolutely free. I understand I am not obligated to join the Silhouette Book Club unless I decide to keep them.

NAME_____

ADDRESS_____

CITY_____ STATE_____ ZIP_____